"We all say Alison's like the Mounties," Lisa said. "She always gets her man!"

Jean-Luc shook his head. "But not this man, Lisa," he said, and looked at her strangely. "Alison will not get *this* man!"

He turned his attention back to the magazine. "And now, Lisa, shall we get back down to work?"

Lisa nodded her head, and resumed her reading. As Jean-Luc turned the pages of *Paris-Match* his bare arm accidentally brushed against the skin of hers. A frisson of delight shot through her.

Suddenly Lisa found it very difficult to concentrate on her work. Indeed, work was now the last thing on her mind.

Also in the Point Romance series:

French Kiss

Robyn Turner

Cover illustration by Derek Brazell

■SCHOLASTIC

Scholastic Children's Books,
Scholastic Publications Ltd,
7–9 Pratt Street, London NW1 0AE, UK

Scholastic Inc.,
555 Broadway, New York, NY 10012-3999, USA

Scholastic Canada Ltd,
123 Newkirk Road, Richmond Hill,
Ontario, Canada L4C 3G5

Ashton Scholastic Pty Ltd,
P O Box 579, Gosford, New South Wales,
Australia

Ashton Scholastic Ltd,
Private Bag 92801, Penrose, Auckland,
New Zealand

First published in the UK by Scholastic Children's Books, 1994

Text copyright © Robyn Turner, 1994
Cover artwork copyright © Derek Brazell, 1994

ISBN 0 590 55415 8

Typeset by TW Typesetting, Midsomer Norton, Avon
Printed by Cox & Wyman Ltd, Reading, Berks.

10 9 8 7 6 5 4 3 2 1

1

"She didn't!"
"She did!"

Lisa Tyler giggled conspiratorially and took off her reading glasses — as if to attend more closely to the lurid story her best friend, Chrissie, was telling her.

Lisa was seventeen now, and with the start of the summer term and mock 'A' levels looming threateningly on the horizon she knew that she ought to be acting in a much more sensible and responsible manner. Her mother, Maddy, had often told her off for listening to and believing idle gossip. But who cared when the gossip was as juicy as this was! And, as Lisa had repeatedly reminded her mother, it was often fun, at which Maddy had laughed and admitted that when she was a sixth-former she too had enjoyed a gossip as much as Lisa.

Lisa glanced behind her at the two scruffy sixth-formers on the back seat of the top floor of the double-decker. They were both engrossed in the latest computer games magazine, which at least meant that they wouldn't be eavesdropping on Chrissie's salacious piece of news.

And that was just as well, Lisa reflected: when it came to keeping secrets boys her age simply weren't to be trusted. Lisa could easily understand why some of her more attractive classmates were going out with boys a year or so older than themselves: at least eighteen- and nineteen-year-olds had that level-headed sense of maturity boys a few years younger lacked.

Lisa was a good-looking girl, whose essential prettiness and big baby-blue eyes were often disguised by her glasses, and the fact that she normally wore her long dark-blonde hair tied tightly back in a pony-tail.

As a science student it was an eminently sensible thing to do, but it did have the unfortunate effect of highlighting the more severe aspects of her face. Nevertheless, when Lisa Tyler smiled — which was often — she could be extraordinarily attractive. She was smiling now as she turned back to Chrissie and urged her to continue her story.

The subject of their whispered discussion was the fate of Eliane, the popular young French student teacher from Paris, who had been working as an assistant at the school for the past two terms. Only a few years older than the pupils she was teaching, the glamorous Frenchwoman had impressed and entertained Lisa and her fellow students with her sophisticated tales of the French capital, and her earthy good humour. French lessons, they all agreed, had suddenly become fun again.

But then, Lisa reminded herself, anyone would have been an improvement on their regular teacher, Mr Crowley, whose frosty ways and imposing manner didn't exactly inspire enthusiasm for 'A' level French in his class of nine girls and five boys.

"So what happened?" Lisa asked Chrissie, eager for more dirt.

Chrissie threw back her long brown hair, and grandly paused for effect before continuing: "So Alison Potter went round to her flat – I reckon she wanted a bit of help with this term's project – and the landlady said she'd disappeared, just packed up her bags and left for France, without so much as a by-your-leave—"

"So who's going to teach us French for the summer term?" Lisa asked automatically.

Chrissie tutted. "Lisa! Must you always be so practical?" she asked, barely concealing her disgust. "There are more important things than schoolwork, you know!"

She shook her head sympathetically, and regarded her best friend. Lisa was a hard worker, there was no doubt about that. After all with French, Chemistry and Biology 'A' levels to study for she had to be. But there were times when Chrissie wished Lisa would let go a little more, and act as a seventeen-year-old girl was *supposed* to act. It had taken practically a war of attrition, Chrissie remembered, to persuade Lisa to go off to the latest hottest disco down in London the other weekend.

On the other hand, Lisa's hard work ensured that in her schoolwork she always got B-plusses and the occasional A. For her part, Chrissie thought it was a cause worthy of major celebration if she managed to scrape through with a B-minus.

Lisa blushed, concealing her awkwardness by replacing her glasses. "Sorry," she said.

Chrissie nodded and continued: "Now you know I'm not one to gossip—"

"Oh yes?" said Lisa, and smiled. Chrissie was genuinely kind-hearted and a loyal friend, but if there was a chance to dish the dirt on anyone then she was always the first in line.

"Well, last term she was off sick a lot during the mornings, and she started to put on weight . . ."

Lisa's eyes widened with delight at the wicked piece of news. She affected a look of being scandalized. "You don't mean . . ."

"Well, she didn't get that fat through eating too many cream cakes and missing the odd aerobics class, now, did she? Lisa, you can be so dim at times!"

Lisa aimed a friendly punch at Chrissie's shoulder. "Unlike you, Chrissie Spence," she said in a mock superior tone, "I don't automatically think the worst of everyone . . . Anyway," she continued, grinning, "I didn't think teachers got up to that sort of thing . . ."

"I suppose they're human, just like the rest of

us," said Chrissie, and shuddered. "What a horrible thought, though . . ."

The bus lurched to a halt outside the gates of Applewood School and Sixth Form College, and Lisa and Chrissie stood up to get off. The two sixth-formers pushed rudely past them and clattered down the stairs. Lisa stuck out her tongue at them. So what if it was childish? she thought; it still felt good. She turned back to Chrissie.

"What is it about the average male student of our age," she asked rhetorically, "which makes him behave like a gorilla just let out of London Zoo, searching for his next banana?"

Chrissie smiled and shrugged. "Who knows, Lisa? But for once wouldn't it be nice to have a gorgeous intelligent hunk come over and just sweep us off our feet, instead of a pimply schoolboy whose mind's only on one thing, and who stinks of cheap aftershave . . ."

"*And* has remembered to clean under his nails," Lisa added, and laughed again. "You're going to have to look a lot further than Applewood if you want that!"

"Yeah, somehow I can't imagine Tom Cruise or a Levi jeans model jetting over and inviting us both out," Chrissie said philosophically. "I suppose we'll have to make do with what we've got . . ." She shook her head sadly and sighed. "Boys! I don't know why we bother with them sometimes . . ."

"I don't," said Lisa pointedly. "I've got too much work to do to have time for a boyfriend . . ."

Chrissie winked at her. "What about James?"

5

"James is *not* my boyfriend," Lisa said defensively and only half-convincingly. "We're just good friends, that's all."

"That's not the impression I got at Christmas—" Chrissie said as they jumped off the bus.

Lisa blushed as she remembered the way her old friend, James, had cornered her at Alison Potter's Christmas party, and the long lingering kiss they had shared under the mistletoe. They'd had a couple of glasses of wine too many, she reminded herself, and in the festivities their kiss hadn't seemed such a bad idea. It certainly hadn't gone any further.

Even if Lisa had wanted it to go further there was no opportunity for it to do so. James had been Lisa's neighbour since they were both children; now, however, he was a first-year student at Manchester University and only returned home in the holidays.

Besides, Lisa had decided that she had no time for boyfriends if she was going to pass her 'A' levels next year and go on to university.

"Oh, it was just one of those things," Lisa said breezily, trying to sound like a woman experienced in the ways of the world, and to cover up her embarrassment at the incident.

"Oh yeah?" Chrissie joked good-naturedly, calling her friend's bluff. "He could be quite a catch, you know, Lisa. He's not bad-looking and when he qualifies he's going to be a rich doctor . . ."

"Doctors aren't rich any more," Lisa riposted, joining in the fun. "Haven't you ever watched

Casualty? Besides, I saw him during the Easter holidays."

"Oh?" Chrissie arched an eyebrow in interest: this was news even to her.

"His mum lives next door — how could I miss him?" Lisa said, before Chrissie could put any significance to the fact.

"It's always the boy next door," Chrissie said wisely, continuing her teasing. "Haven't *you* watched any of the daytime soaps?"

"Do you know what James does in his spare time?" Lisa asked and added grimly: "You're not going to like it . . ."

"I'm not?" Chrissie asked eagerly.

Lisa nodded sadly, enjoying teasing her friend. "When I first found out I have to admit it shook me up a bit," she said solemnly, and shuddered.

Chrissie couldn't wait to hear. She imagined all sorts of filthy habits and twisted perversions: who would have thought it of good old innocuous James? It was always the quiet ones, her dad had said every Sunday from behind his copy of the *News of the World*.

"Well, come on. Tell me!" she said, stamping her foot impatiently even though they could hear the ringing of the bell, signalling the start of morning classes.

"Are you sure you really want to know?" asked Lisa, relishing Chrissie's exasperation.

"For goodness' sake, Lisa, just tell me!"

Lisa drew Chrissie to one side, and leant over confidentially to her ear.

"Well, he told me that when he's not working

7

he likes to—" Lisa shook her head, and shuddered — "he likes to go—"

"Yes?" Chrissie was agog.

Lisa took a long deep breath: "Well, he likes to go *train-spotting*!"

Chrissie shivered with revulsion. "Ugh, gross!" she said with feeling, and raced Lisa up the hill which led to Applewood College.

The sky was grey and threatening and they splashed through the puddles from the previous evening's thunderstorm. This sort of weather was only to be expected: it was, after all, the first day of the summer term.

2

Applewood School and Sixth-Form College was much like any other school anywhere in the country. Applewood was a small modern town about fifty minutes' journey north of London, and the college was underfunded, understaffed, and overstretched. Still, alone among all the colleges in the area, it did have a good reputation, especially for languages.

This was due, in part, to Miss Bailey, the principal, who ensured that, no matter how tight the budget was, every year assistant teachers from France, Germany and Italy would come to the school to help the language teachers. Contact with native speakers was invaluable, Miss Bailey insisted, especially as the linguistic experience of some of the teachers at school was questionable, to say the least.

Lisa had once said that the closest Mr Crowley – inevitably rechristened Creepy Crowley by his classes – had ever been to the real France was the

9

hypermarket at Boulogne; it was an uncharacteristically cynical remark on Lisa's behalf; but it was also absolutely true.

These assistants were usually students from foreign colleges who were studying to be teachers themselves, and were very often no more than a few years older than the pupils they were teaching.

Because of the similarity in age, the students found the assistant teachers much more approachable; many of the girls, for instance, had asked Eliane for help in their essays, or just chatted to her about their problems with boyfriends, or asked for make-up tips. Several of the more daring boys had even asked her out on dates. Eliane maintained that she always refused, although some of the older boys had let it be known that they had joined her for a drink once or twice at one of the local trendy wine bars.

Since her first trip to France four years ago, Lisa had fallen in love with the French and their culture. On a school tour to Normandy and Britanny, she had marvelled at the towering gothic splendours of the great Mont Saint Michel, and the magnificent cathedrals of Rouen, and Caen, where William the Conqueror was buried.

The charming narrow streets of the small towns seemed always to be filled with cheerful people, intent on enjoying life to the fullest. Their smiling faces, their long lunches spent outside on pavement cafés, their taking nothing seriously had all appealed to the hard-working Lisa, and they all seemed to exude a certain sort of innate style, even when wearing just jeans and a T-shirt.

The ready wit of the Breton peasant had charmed her as much as her cooking, and even though she knew that the people in the north of France were very different from their more sophisticated cousins in Paris, or on the Riviera in the south, Lisa still felt a strange affinity with the country.

It was this love for all things French which had inspired her to study the language at 'A' level – a particularly odd combination with her other two subjects of Chemistry and Biology. Her teachers had advised her against it, recommending her to do a third science subject instead, but Lisa had insisted: only by studying the language would she ever gain a proper understanding of the French and their way of life, she had said.

"You know, Lisa," Chrissie had teased her at the time, "that was probably the most exciting thing you've done in your entire life!"

And this is probably the most boring thing I've ever done in my life, Lisa thought glumly as she sat at her desk listening to Mr Crowley droning on in that monotonous voice of his about some obscure and minute point of French grammar, a detail she'd probably never have the opportunity to put into practice.

She looked around at her classmates. Chrissie was just as bored as she was and was doodling on the back of her notebook. They exchanged a look of mutual despair, and silently agreed that French lessons had been much more fun when Eliane had been talking about trendy Parisian life, and teaching them some of the juicier words of French slang.

At the back of the class Alison Potter was busy passing a note under her desk to the boy sitting next to her. Alison, with her red hair and startling green eyes, was one of the most popular girls at Applewood, and widely known as the school flirt. Her enemies – who were all less attractive than her, of course – said that if you were male, and had a pulse, then Alison would be interested in you. It was only half-true, Lisa knew, but there was no doubt that Alison enjoyed the company of men: she had actually flirted with a couple of the younger and more attractive teachers, although even Alison would stop at the fifty-year-old Mr Crowley. Lisa and Alison weren't exactly friends but Lisa had to admit to a sneaking envious admiration for her brash and forthright fellow student.

In front of her, even Stuart, the too-good-to-be-true blue-eyed blond who, much to the distress of the entire female contingent of the college, had been going steady with Helen Wilkinson for as long as anyone could remember, was staring blankly into space. If he, who always gets straight As, can't take this much longer, thought Lisa, then what hope is there for the rest of us?

Lisa stared out of the window across the playground and at the staff car park, where all the teachers' cars were waiting in the pouring rain. As Crowley droned on about the finer points of the past preterite tense of the verb *s'ennuyer* – which means to be bored, which is exactly what I am at the moment, she realized – Lisa looked idly at each of the cars, trying to identify their owners and thinking how aptly each one matched its owner's personality.

There was the grey Ford Escort belonging to Mr Ward, the English teacher, as grey and unreliable as the old codger was himself; the pushbike of the vegetarian, eco-friendly, no-smoking, no-drinking, no-anything art teacher; and the mud-brown Mini of the tiny Miss Edwardes, whose explanations of advanced computer programming were indeed about as clear as mud.

All as drab and as colourless as their owners, and this typical English summer's day, thought Lisa as she peered out through the pouring rain up at the bleak and ironically wintry sky.

There was however one car which she didn't recognize: parked somewhat inexpertly between two parking bays, and with a total disregard for allotted parking spaces, was a battered car which Lisa could only describe as an upturned rusty tin bath on wheels.

It was sprayed bright green, bringing a little touch of colour to the dreary car park. Or at least most of the car was sprayed bright green. The doors were white, as though they were left-overs from another car which had been grafted on to it.

Lisa recognized the car as a Citroen 2CV, the cheap, noisy but nevertheless reliable car much loved of university students, and people too poor to afford anything else. In France, she recalled, it was known as a *Deux Chevaux*.

She wondered who the car might belong to, and looked around for other clues; in the background, Creepy Crowley's dreary voice droned on and on.

13

He was still talking about the verb *s'ennuyer*. Why doesn't he start on *s'endormir* — to fall asleep — thought Lisa; because that's what we're all going to do if he doesn't stop soon!

The boot of the 2CV was plastered with stickers from French towns — Cannes, Nice, Marseilles, Paris — and several Lisa had never heard of before, and just above the bumper, at a particularly askew angle, was a large white circle in the middle of which was the letter 'F'. Lisa realized instantly that the car must belong to the new French assistant, who had probably travelled by road all the way from her home town to Applewood.

Well, at least with a car like that she's bound to be more fun than Creepy's boring verbs and past tenses, Lisa thought optimistically, and returned to her lesson.

"Well, has anyone seen her yet?" the bespectacled and pimply Simon Waites asked eagerly, as he, Lisa, Chrissie and Alison sat around in the Common Room during their free period. He was chewing on a piece of gum, as he swaggered up to them, hands hooked in the belt loops of his jeans.

Simon, with his leather jacket, white T-shirt, black 501s, slicked-back hair and an earring in his right ear, thought he looked the epitome of cool. It came from watching too many rock 'n' roll movies with his dad, Lisa had long ago decided, but realized that there was something casually endearing about him. Chrissie had agreed with her: if Simon would only stop pretending that he had been born in a 1950s rock 'n' roll musical he might even have something going for him. After all, he wasn't bad-looking in a gawky sort of way.

"Has anyone checked her out yet?" he repeated in his fake American drawl.

"Seen who?" asked Alison, and glanced up from reading her horoscope in that month's issue of *Cosmopolitan*. It forecast that Alison would meet a tall dark handsome stranger, which, knowing Alison, was hardly surprising. She accorded the irksome Simon the same sort of look she usually reserved for a newly-discovered colony of blackheads.

"The new French assistant, of course!" he said.

"And why would she interest you?" Chrissie asked evilly, joining in the fun.

Simon licked his lips eagerly. "Well, you know what they say about French women . . ."

"No, *we don't*," said Lisa, and winked complicitly at her two companions. "Tell us, Simon, what *do* they say?"

Simon blushed and lowered his gaze but the three girls rounded gleefully on him and urged him to continue.

"Well. She's bound to be glamorous and sophisticated," he said. "And she's a stranger here, and she's going to want someone to show her around the place, maybe take her up West to a movie, or a club . . ."

"And of course *you'd* fit the bill perfectly, Si?" asked Lisa.

Simon shrugged his shoulders in a nonchalant

15

hey-I'm-a-man-of-the-world gesture. "Hey, if the chick wants an escort who am I to refuse . . ."

Chrissie winced at Simon's use of what he thought was current American slang: he'd obviously been watching too many old American sit-coms on TV. One day, she decided, she would have to take him aside and give him some words of well-meaning advice.

Lisa, meanwhile, just smiled to herself. The idea of Simon Waites taking a sophisticated and beautiful young Frenchwoman for a night out in London's West End was about as likely as her getting an A double-plus in Biology. Still, *she* could talk: when was the last time a handsome hunk had taken *her* out for dinner?

"Simon," said Alison, from behind her copy of *Cosmo*, "if a woman ever actually agreed to go out with you for a night then she'd either have to be mad, or blind—"

"Or your sister," finished Chrissie, "and even then she'd have to be hard up."

Simon's face fell and he looked ruefully at the two girls before slinking away.

When he'd gone, Lisa light-heartedly reproved Chrissie and Alison for their actions. Admittedly, there were times when Simon could make a complete idiot of himself – and he could also be big-headed in the extreme – but did they have to be so truthful?

"You're too soft, Lisa," Chrissie said, even though she was feeling a little guilty. "Si's like all boys his age. He thinks he's God's gift . . ."

"Maybe he's just shy," Lisa said charitably. She

liked to think that she could sum up people pretty well: and she thought she saw, behind Si's posturing and affected coolness, someone who was very unsure of himself and who just wanted to be liked. "When you're our age, it's expected of us that we should all be going out with someone."

"You're not," Alison pointed out. "And neither is Chrissie."

"I'm too picky," Chrissie said, in a bitchy tone which implied that Alison, whose boyfriend of the week was the captain of the football team from a neighbouring college, wasn't; "And Lisa's too busy with her schoolwork to be bothered with anything so mundane as *boys*."

Lisa glowered at her friend: Chrissie wasn't meaning to be unkind, but nevertheless the comment stung. Certainly Lisa had to admit that she was involved with her schoolwork to such an extent that it did hurt her social life. She always got good grades but it wasn't because of any natural intelligence – like Stuart, for instance; what she achieved was through nothing less than hours and hours of sheer hard work.

Nor was Chrissie right when she said that Lisa wasn't interested in having a boyfriend. The truth was that Lisa would have loved to be going out with someone. She was popular with the boys, there was no doubt about that; but when it came to girlfriends most of the boys at Applewood seemed only to be interested in the glamorous, outward-going girls, like Alison.

Girls like Lisa who were reasonably good-looking but still wouldn't stand out in a crowd were treated as little more than surrogate big sisters, or good mates.

"Boys our age are, like, really superficial," Chrissie had once told her during a heart-to-heart chat. "If you don't look like Demi Moore or Madonna then they're not interested. All they want is to be seen with a trophy on their arm: they don't care about the person underneath."

Lisa shrugged; there would be enough time for boys in the summer holidays and when she'd finished her 'A' levels. She attempted to change the subject.

"So what do you think the new French assistant will be like?" she asked.

Alison shrugged. "As long as she tells me how to chat up French boys when I go on holiday to Paris I'll be happy," she said brightly and returned to her magazine.

"Be serious, Alison!" said Lisa.

"If it's a choice between being serious and being driven down the Champs Elysées by Jean-Michel Jarre you know which one I'd take . . ."

"No, it's important," insisted Lisa. "A good foreign languages assistant can really improve our spoken French, and help push up our grades."

At the same time Lisa realized that Alison was right and she was indeed being a little too earnest for her own good. Maybe that was why the boys didn't take such an interest in her?

"No one could be as much fun as Eliane," said Chrissie. "With our luck the new assistant will be over fifty, be as boring as old Creepy Crowley, and stink of garlic." She giggled. "She'll have as much dress sense as a scarecrow, and she probably won't even shave under her arms . . ."

"Well, we'll soon find out," said Lisa, as the bell rang and she picked up her books to go to her Chemistry lesson. "We'll be meeting her tomorrow in the French class."

"I can't wait . . ." said Chrissie sarcastically.

3

"*Bonjour, mes élèves*," announced Crowley the following day in his heavily-accented French. "*Permettez-moi de vous présenter votre nouveau assistant français . . .*"

A collective silent sigh of surprise and appreciation went up from most of the girls in the room (and, it has to be admitted, from one of the boys). Each one of them was taken aback; each, that is, except Lisa whose ready ear and linguistic knowledge had caught in Crowley's introduction the vital difference between the expected feminine *assistante française*, and the unquestionably masculine *assistant français* who had just walked into the room.

"OK, I take it all back," Chrissie whispered to Lisa. "The new French assistant isn't over fifty . . ."

Lisa nodded in agreement, and peered through her glasses at the newcomer. "Not even over twenty-five," she said.

"Isn't over fifty?" said red-headed Alison who had given up on yesterday's flirting with the boy at the back of class, and was now sitting on the other side of Lisa. "Hey, she isn't even a she!"

"No one's going to argue with you there, Alison," Lisa agreed.

Dressed casually but stylishly in Chipie blue jeans, and a red Chevignon sweatshirt, the new French assistant could have easily passed for the elder brother of any one of the students in the class.

He was about twenty-one, tall and slim, with broad shoulders, and the taut firm body of a swimmer. A shock of thick jet-black hair curled over his collar and his swarthy good looks were further accentuated by a deep tan, and a mischievous twinkle which glittered behind his deep brown eyes.

"Je vous présente Monsieur Jean-Luc Roupie," announced Crowley.

"Oooh-la-la," whistled Alison in the only French she could pronounce perfectly.

Unfortunately she said it just a little too loudly, and Jean-Luc heard her. He looked around the class and met Alison's admiring gaze, and smiled a nervous and embarrassed smile.

With those wonderful white teeth, Lisa found herself thinking, and prodded Alison in the side.

"Behave yourself, Alison!" she reproved in a harsh whisper.

"Bonjour, mademoiselle," Jean-Luc grinned, and winked at Alison, calling the girl's bluff. Alison flushed briefly with embarrassment before

responding with her own mumbled *"Bonjour, monsieur."*

"Please," the Frenchman said, "there is no need to be so formal with me. You can call me Jean-Luc." It seemed eminently sensible to the entire class: Jean-Luc, after all, couldn't have been more than three or four years older than any of them.

While Crowley continued to introduce Jean-Luc to the class, Alison licked her lips, and continued appreciating the handsome French assistant from the top of his thick black hair to the tips of his polished trendy cowboy boots.

"I want that," she stated firmly, and only half-jokingly.

Lisa pretended to look shocked but couldn't suppress a snigger. "Alison, don't you ever think of anything else?" she asked.

"No," Alison replied happily, and continued to drool over the young Frenchman standing at the front of the class.

"Bonjour, la classe," Jean-Luc addressed them in a voice as deep brown as his eyes. Lisa noticed that it trembled just a little. She had the impression that Jean-Luc was slightly nervous, and realized just how intimidating a whole classroom full of strangers would appear to a student teacher only recently arrived from a foreign country.

And who'd blame him? she thought sympathetically. Facing thirteen 'A' level students – and Alison Potter! It's enough to give anyone nightmares!

"I thank Monsieur Crowley for the introduction," he continued, still speaking in French, although a little too quickly for several members of the class to be able to follow him. "Let me tell you a little about myself. I come from the town of Cannes—"

"Can anyone tell me where that is?" Crowley butted in, his spoken French, with its heavy English intonation, contrasting sharply with Jean-Luc's natural accent.

Everyone knew where the famous Riviera town of Cannes was of course, but, as the question was asked in French, thereby requiring an answer in French, few put their hands up.

Two who did, however, were Lisa and Stuart. Crowley ignored Stuart – who, he knew, would give the correct answer and in a French so faultless that it would put his to shame – and instead encouraged Lisa to answer.

"Eh bien, Mademoiselle Tyler?"

"Cannes se trouve au sud-est de la France, monsieur," Lisa answered, *"sur la plage."*

She realized self-consciously just how un-French her accent must sound to a native like Jean-Luc. Well, at least my grammar's correct, she consoled herself.

By Crowley's side, Jean-Luc secretly grinned: if everyone's French accents were as bad as Crowley and Lisa's then he was going to have his work cut out for him this summer term!

Still, Jean-Luc beamed encouragingly at the shy and unsure girl in the spectacles who had answered the question. *"Très bien, mademoiselle,"* he said, congratulating her, *"tu parles français très bien!"*

Lisa muttered an awkward *merci* and found herself blushing and feeling a little awkward under Jean-Luc's gaze. It felt pleasantly odd to be congratulated on her skill at French. Creepy Crowley never praised any of his students: and praise to Lisa was what water was to a thirsty man.

Congratulating her on her answer Jean-Luc continued to talk about himself, with such a speed and pronounced regional accent that only the very brightest could keep up with him. Crowley noted this: he would have to take Jean-Luc aside later and ask him to slow down in future; otherwise no one — including himself — would be able to follow him.

"Cannes," Chrissie sighed dreamily as soon as Lisa had sat down. "Long golden beaches on the Riviera, the Film Festival, azure-blue oceans, palm trees . . ."

"Why would someone want to leave all that to come here?" Lisa asked rhetorically and pointed out through the classroom window at the grey skies and thudding rain of another typically English summer day.

"The Riviera must be where he got his tan," gushed Alison, who had decided that Jean-Luc was going to be her sole topic of conversation for the rest of the day. "Lying on the beach all day, sipping Pernod . . . occasionally taking time off from his yacht moored in the harbour to go swimming or windsurfing and develop those well-toned muscles of his . . ."

"How do you know he's got muscles?" asked Chrissie. "We've only just seen him for the first time! And he's wearing a baggy sweatshirt!"

"Anyone that hunky has got to have muscles," Alison replied categorically. "Don't you know anything?"

"Alison, be serious!" laughed Lisa. "He's a student. He's as poor as we are and probably spends most of his time sitting in a dingy old library, reading boring text books, and working on a dissertation!"

Beside her Chrissie sighed. "Lisa, haven't you got any sense of romance at all?"

"I'm just being realistic, Chrissie," Lisa pointed out, a little too primly for her own good.

"Boring more like it!" Chrissie smiled fondly at her old friend. "Still, you've got to admit he's a bit of a good-looker, isn't he?"

Lisa pretended to consider the Frenchman for a moment. "He's all right, if you like that sort of thing . . ." she said begrudgingly, and, in response to Chrissie's challenging look of utter disbelief, added: "Well, OK, he's more than all right."

"Aha!" Alison crowed triumphantly. "Lisa Tyler has feelings and urges and drives! She finally admits to being just like the rest of us mere mortals!"

"He's also our teacher," Lisa continued with a wry smile. "If you think he's ever going to look at us as anything other than his pupils then you're going to be disappointed, Alison!"

"Mademoiselle Tyler!" came Crowley's stern

voice. "Will you stop gossiping and attend to the lesson please!"

"Oui, Monsieur Crowley," she sighed, and looked reproachfully at Alison. Once again her man-mad fellow student had got her into trouble: the last time had been when Alison had persuaded her to pass a note to a student in the upper sixth whom she wanted to get to know. The boy's girlfriend had seen her do it and had assumed that it was Lisa who was after him: there had been an awful lot of explaining to do that day.

"Pay no attention to Creepy Crowley," Alison whispered to Lisa, after Jean-Luc had left the classroom, and the older teacher had set them some written work. "Listen . . . you're good at French, aren't you?"

"I'm OK," Lisa said modestly. "I get my Bs and the occasional A-minus."

"You're better than me, anyway," admitted Alison. "So do me a favour and translate this for me."

Making sure that Crowley wasn't looking Alison passed a small piece of paper over to Lisa.

"Don't you think that Stuart would be better at this?" asked Lisa, without reading the note and instead nodding towards the good-looking blond at the front of the class whose head was buried deep in his text book.

"No way," hissed Alison, and urged Lisa to look at the note. "This is really important girls' stuff!"

Intrigued, Lisa opened the folded note, and read: Hello there, gorgeous, has anyone ever told you that you have the cutest smile and the most gorgeous eyes this side of the English Channel?

"You want me to translate this into French?" Lisa asked in amazement.

Alison nodded furiously: she was going to get a date with Jean-Luc if it was the last thing she did.

Lisa sighed and raised her eyes heavenwards. Something told her that it was going to be an eventful summer term . . .

4

"So are you still thinking of asking the new French teacher out on a date, Si?" Lisa asked mischievously the following morning as she, Simon and Chrissie sat around in the common room, waiting for the start of classes.

"I seem to remember you promised you'd be the first one to take 'her' on a wild night out," Chrissie added evilly.

Simon flushed a very vivid shade of red. "Hey, c'mon, girls, leave me alone . . ." he stuttered, with embarrassment. "I was only foolin' y'know . . . he's a guy after all . . ."

"Any old excuse," said Chrissie, and sniffed haughtily, less at Simon's reply and more at his irritating and obviously fake American accent.

"Some people just don't have the courage of their convictions," giggled Lisa, and returned to the science book she was reading.

"Don't you ever lighten up, Lisa?" Chrissie teased and pointed down at Lisa's text book.

"This is the common room! You can get away without doing any work here!"

Lisa smiled. "I've got to get the grades if I'm going to go to university," she reminded her.

Chrissie shook her head. "You're dedicated, Lisa, I'll give you that," she said in admiration. "Once you set your mind to something there's no stopping you." She sighed. "As for me, well, just one episode of an Aussie soap and that's my homework gone for the night . . ."

Lisa laughed and was about to return to her reading when the door of the common room opened. Simon whistled appreciatively at the figure who was walking into the room; even Lisa and Chrissie had to look twice.

"Will you just look at that?" he gasped.

"I'd rather not," riposted Lisa, and grinned. "It's hurting my eyes . . ."

Alison had just entered the room, and was dressed to kill in an ultra-short skirt which revealed her long shapely legs, and a tight top which did much the same for her attributes above the waist.

Her red hair was freshly washed, and cascaded behind her as she bounced over to Lisa and the others. Few of the boys could keep their eyes off her; and not a girl in the room could resist glaring at her.

She sat down and grinned at Lisa and Chrissie. Chrissie looked pointedly at her watch.

"It's nine o'clock in the morning, Alison," she said.

"So?"

"The night-clubs don't open for another twelve hours or so . . ."

"What do you mean?" asked Alison, knowing exactly what they meant.

Lisa smiled. "Don't you think you're just a little overdressed for school, Alison?" she asked, and looked critically at Alison's short skirt. Underdressed is more like it! she thought and looked down at her own plain but practical sloppy sweatshirt and jeans, which seemed to be the standard uniform of most students at Applewood.

Alison affected a look of disappointment at her friends. "What's wrong with a girl taking a little bit of pride in her appearance?" she asked.

"This wouldn't have anything to do with a certain Frenchman, would it?" Lisa asked with a knowing twinkle in her eye.

"Of course not," said Alison, convincing no one, and continued nonchalantly: "But all Frenchmen are notorious for their appreciation of feminine charms. And who am I to disappoint this one?" She adjusted her appearance in the reflection of one of the windows. "After all, we want to make his stay in our country as pleasant as possible, don't we?"

Lisa laughed and stood up and collected her books as the bell for her first class of the morning rang. Alison was good-looking, there was no doubt about that; and more to the point, she had so much total and absolute confidence in herself that very few boys could resist her charms.

If anyone of them was likely to make a date

with the handsome Jean-Luc then it was bound to be her. She and Chrissie, and all the others, even if they had wanted to, didn't stand a chance in the face of that competition!

"OK, come on, Alison," Chrissie challenged as she stood up to join Lisa. "Let's see you in action . . . it's French conversation now. Let's see you work your charms on Jean-Luc!"

Alison swanned into the French classroom with all the style and grace of a Hollywood beauty queen at a movie première. All the boys looked at her in admiration, and all the girls winked knowingly at each other.

As soon as the early-morning hubbub had faded down and everyone had taken their seats, Jean-Luc walked into the classroom, carrying his books under his arm. He was wearing blue jeans, and a freshly laundered and brilliantly white open-necked shirt, which shone in the nine o'clock sunlight streaming in through the high classroom windows.

As Lisa opened her text book she found herself idly wondering who it was who ironed and washed Jean-Luc's shirts. Looking around at the other boys in the class, with their scruffy and crumpled T-shirts, most of which also carried the remains of this morning's breakfast, you would have been forgiven for thinking that no male under the age of twenty-five knew what a washing machine or a steam iron was, let alone how to operate them.

But hey, he's French, she realized, and all the

French, men and women alike, always make sure that they look good. Why should I presume that it's his girlfriend who irons his shirt? It could just as easily be his landlady. Or even himself! He is French after all!

And Lisa suddenly wondered why the identity of the person who ironed Jean-Luc's shirts mattered so much to her.

It's a great shirt though, she concluded, trying to change her track of thought. Classic French simplicity and elegance, which goes so well with his tanned complexion, and really sets off his dark hair.

And then she pleasantly surprised and shocked herself by adding: and those tiny chest hairs creeping over the tiny 'V' in the open neck and which look so cute . . .

Jean-Luc thumped his books down on the teacher's desk, and turned to face the class. The smile with which he greeted the class suddenly changed to a look of pleasant and interested surprise as his normally mischievous brown eyes took in the sight before him.

Alison was sitting right in the centre desk of the front row, after having unceremoniously kicked out its usual occupant to the back of the class. She was gazing seductively at Jean-Luc with her dazzlingly green eyes.

She flickered her eyelids alluringly at the young French assistant as he moved around the classroom, as though he was the only thing which mattered in the entire world. It was a routine which Alison had played many times before with some of the boys from the upper sixth, and it was a routine which had never once failed.

Jean-Luc, intensely aware of Alison's attention, flushed with embarrassment, and looked to the board as if for moral support. He announced that he was going to tell them a little more about his home town of Cannes and drew their attention to a large wall map of France, and asked the class, in French, if any of them could point out the location of the coastal town.

Several hands went up, but it was Alison who stood up and left her desk and sashayed slowly over to the map for the benefit of Jean-Luc. A few of the girls giggled at her audacity, but there was no doubt that Jean-Luc was impressed: he gazed admiringly at Alison's slim figure, as she tried to locate Cannes on the map.

Lisa found herself scowling enviously at her flirtatious colleague. Does she have to make it so obvious? she growled to herself. We know she's got everything going for her – and Jean-Luc's no better either, getting an eyeful of her! He shouldn't encourage her!

Alison frowned, searching the south-eastern coastline of France for the town. Finally she found it and with a look of triumph on her face pointed out the town nestling on the Côte d'Azur and looking out over the warm waters of the Mediterranean sea. She glanced over at Jean-Luc for approval; he was beaming at her.

"*Très bien, Mademoiselle . . . Mademoiselle . . . ?*" he asked, having forgotten her name.

"*Je m'appelle Alison,*" she said huskily, in an

accent which was about as French as a plate of fish and chips.

Jean-Luc smiled. *"D'accord,"* he said. *"Très bien, Alison."*

Alison turned round to rejoin the class with a look of triumph on her face, as if to say: Round one to me, folks, and Jean-Luc switched into English.

"Now who can tell me the best way one can travel to Cannes?" he asked, in his deep-brown French accent.

"That's easy," piped up Chrissie, who had been to the South of France on holiday some years ago. "You take the plane down to Nice, and then get a train into town."

Jean-Luc's eyes twinkled. "That might be the quickest way, Chrissie," he said, and Chrissie smiled as he remembered her name. "But without doubt it is not the best," he continued. "The flight down to Cannes is most expensive – *très cher.* Poor college students like yourself" – and here he smiled – "and even university students like myself who are much more poorer cannot afford such luxury. No, we must travel by train, and in that way we can also see all the beauties of my great country: the mountains of the Haute-Savoie region, the châteaux of the Loire valley, the rolling hills of the Midi . . ."

"I know the sort of French beauties I'd like to see," Alison whispered to Lisa.

"Alison! Behave!" hissed Lisa, and kicked her on the shin.

Jean-Luc switched back to French and regarded Lisa. *"Alors, Mademoiselle . . . Mademoiselle . . ."*

"Lisa," she offered. Damn! Why does he have to remember Chrissie's name and not mine! she thought.

"Bon, Lisa," he continued in French, and asked her to come to the front of the class. "So let us pretend that you are a tourist in Paris and you want to come to Cannes . . ."

Lisa nodded nervously and stood up and left her desk. She hated these role-playing games where she had to stand in front of the class; she felt so self-conscious and worried that she would make a fool of herself in front of her classmates.

Jean-Luc was well aware of this, of course; ever since she had answered Mr Crowley's question on the first day of term he had realized that Lisa was a potentially good French speaker, who merely lacked the confidence to express herself properly.

Lisa took a deep breath and looked over at Jean-Luc's encouraging and smiling face. He seemed to be saying, Don't worry, just ignore everyone else in the class. Just pretend that there's only you and me.

"Excuse me, monsieur," Lisa began in faltering touristy French. "Could you give me the directions to the railway station?"

Jean-Luc rubbed his chin thoughtfully with a long-fingered – and ringless – hand, before replying.

"Aha, so you want the directions to the Gare du Nord, mademoiselle?" he asked, referring to one of Paris' railway stations with a mischievous gleam in his eyes – a gleam which Lisa missed.

"Oui, c'est ça!" she said, and a brief conversation took place between them in which Jean-Luc told Lisa which Metro line to take to the Gare du Nord from where she could then catch her train.

Even though Lisa made several grammatical and pronunciation mistakes, the conversation went along surprisingly smoothly. The young Frenchman seemed able to put Lisa very much at her ease, and soon she could almost believe that she was a tourist in Paris asking information from a real-life Parisian.

Finally the dialogue ended, and Lisa returned to her seat.

"Excellent, mademoiselle Lisa!" Jean-Luc encouraged, and Lisa felt her breast swell with pride until he added: "There was just one tiny problem though . . ."

Lisa frowned, as did several other members of the class for whom Lisa's performance had been an impressive one.

"And what was that – Jean-Luc?" she asked.

"You wanted to go to Cannes, and yet you let me give you directions to the Gare du Nord railway station," he said.

"So?"

"Like London, Paris has many railway stations, each one of which services a different part of the country," he explained. "If you had wanted to go to the South of France you should have gone to the Gare de Lyon. Catch a train at the Gare du Nord and you would find yourself getting off in Germany!"

The class exploded into laughter and Lisa

glared at Jean-Luc, not realizing that he and the class were laughing not at her but with her. Jean-Luc noticed her look and instantly realized his *faux pas*; he clapped his hands together for silence.

"It's no problem," he said, and smiled kindly at Lisa. "When I left London to come to Applewood College I got on a train at Paddington station – I nearly ended up in Cornwall!"

The class laughed again and this time Lisa joined in. Jean-Luc looked at her and winked conspiratorially; she smiled back. They both knew that it was a lie told for Lisa's benefit, and that Jean-Luc would have travelled to Applewood in the tiny green 2CV which she had seen parked outside in the car park a few days ago. At the same time she knew that Jean-Luc would never ever purposefully set out to hurt her, or indeed anyone else.

There was something about Jean-Luc that Lisa rather liked.

5

Lisa's mother, Maddy, banged furiously at the bathroom door of their two-bedroomed house and looked down at her watch. It was quarter to eight. If her daughter didn't get out of the bathroom now she would make her late for work — not to mention herself late for school.

Lisa, who normally only spent fifteen minutes in the bathroom every morning had now been in there for almost forty minutes. She'd been doing this for the past week and it was beginning to annoy Maddy.

"Come on, Lisa, be fair on me!" she pleaded. "I do have a job to go to, you know!"

"All right, all right, I'm coming," came Lisa's annoyed voice. Her mother was only about twenty years older than her, and certainly looked much younger, with her short-cut hair and trendy sweatshirts and jeans; but there were, however, times when she could come on annoyingly like — well, annoyingly like a mother.

The bathroom door clicked open, and Maddy was hit by the wave of moist heat flowing out of the room from Lisa's bath. Maddy nodded meaningfully towards the shower.

"I just felt like taking a long bath again this morning," Lisa explained in response to her mother's unspoken criticism. "I felt like pampering myself for a change . . ."

Maddy looked suspiciously at her daughter, who normally only took long hot baths when she'd been persuaded by Chrissie and the others to do so and to go out for the night. And even then, Lisa had always said, showers were much more efficient and wasted far less time, time which could be spent doing much more useful things.

Maddy remembered when she had been a teenager way back in the seventies: she had loved long luxurious baths then, the tub filled to the very top with foaming suds and exotic bath oils. She seemed to have spent most of her college days soaking up those rich warm waters and making herself look attractive; which was probably why she had ended up getting such cute boyfriends and such bad grades.

If she had taken two-minute showers like Lisa normally did, rather than hour-long baths, maybe her final degree would have been better and she wouldn't be working now as little more than a glorified secretary in a computer company, trying to support herself and Lisa on one person's wage.

Lisa's face was flushed from her hot bath, and her wet hair was loose and dark and poured down her back. She smelt differently too and Maddy guessed that Lisa had surreptitiously borrowed some of her own eau de toilette.

Maddy continued to regard her daughter suspiciously, but decided not to press the subject. For one thing, there wasn't enough time: if she was late for the office again she'd be in for it!

"Have you done all your homework from last night, Lisa?" she asked as she entered the bathroom.

"Homework?" said Lisa guiltily as she crossed the corridor to her bedroom. "Oh, there's just a little bit of Biology left over . . . I can do that on the bus into school . . ."

Maddy arched an eyebrow in surprise and concern. Lisa was usually conscientious to a fault: it wasn't like her to leave her homework to the last minute like this.

"That's not like you, darling . . ."

Lisa winced under her mother's reproving gaze. "I was reading this book last night, and I suppose I must have got carried away," she said sheepishly.

"And what book's that?" asked Maddy. Knowing her daughter's determination to do well in her exams it was probably some very weighty scientific tome filled with words she, as a mere child of the seventies, couldn't even pronounce, let alone understand.

"It's a French book I borrowed from the library," Lisa offered, "and it's all about this young girl who falls in love with an older man on the Riviera, y'know in the south of France . . .

40

You ought to read it, Mum, it's really sad . . ."

Maddy sighed and shook her head. Lisa might not even realize it herself, but there was very definitely something going on.

And if someone had told Maddy that that something was six feet tall, with dark brown eyes, a Mediterranean complexion, and a distinctly French accent, then she wouldn't have been in the slightest bit surprised.

Lisa found she was humming happily to herself and there was an unaccustomed bounce in her step as she walked down the corridors to her Chemistry class, threading her way in and out of the hordes of students moving from classroom to classroom in the break between lessons.

A few boys stopped to look at her, as if begrudging her her right to be so happy, but for once Lisa didn't mind them staring; it was rare enough that they did, she thought to herself.

She was in a good mood; after all, outside the sun was shining and it seemed that the summer had finally arrived. To celebrate, she was wearing a medium-length white skirt she had picked up in last year's sales and a trendy mint-green Chevignon shirt which set off her dark blonde hair perfectly.

As she was about to turn into the Chemistry laboratory she heard someone call her name. She turned to see Jean-Luc waving at her from the other end of the passageway, and she shoved her way through the crowd towards him.

"Bonjour, Lisa," he said, and smiled.

"Bonjour, monsieur . . . er, *Jean-Luc,"* she said. Somehow it felt odd calling Jean-Luc by his first name, Lisa realized; which was stupid, as she had never felt awkward in calling his predecessor, Eliane, by her first name.

"I hope you have no hard feelings about my playing my little trick on you the other day?" he asked in English.

"Well . . ." Lisa tried to be stern; after all, for several seconds in the class Jean-Luc had made her feel like a prize fool in front of all her friends until she, too, had seen the joke.

Jean-Luc pouted and lowered his head, looking pleadingly at her from under his finely-lashed eyelids.

Just like a naughty puppy begging for a bone, Lisa thought, and discovered that she couldn't resist the Frenchman's playful expression.

"Of course not, Jean-Luc," she said and returned his smile, before adding pointedly: "And it'll probably come in handy when I finally do go to Paris – at least then I'll know which train station to go to!"

"And especially will you know where to catch the train which will take you down to all the millionaires on the Riviera," Jean-Luc continued with his good-natured teasing. He smelt fresh, of roses and soap and starched white shirts; it was quite a change from the cheap aftershave worn by most of the sixth-form boys.

Lisa laughed self-deprecatingly. "Millionaires? Me?" she scoffed. "The closest I'm ever going to get to a millionaire on the Riviera is if he wants someone to work as a cleaner on his yacht. And even then he'd have to pay my train fare to get me down there!"

"You shouldn't put yourself down so, Lisa," Jean-Luc rebuked her gently, and his normally mischievous deep brown eyes suddenly turned darkly serious. "If you do it often enough you will end up with yourself believing it."

Lisa flinched involuntarily under the young Frenchman's steady gaze. Jean-Luc had touched a raw nerve. Ever since she had been little Lisa had always considered herself somehow not quite as good as the other girls in her class.

Perhaps it was something to do with her father dying and leaving her and her mother when she was eleven, while all the other kids were part of big happy families – or so it seemed at the time. But ever since then Lisa had always been painfully aware of what she imagined to be her own shortcomings, and, to ease the pain, had made a joke of it.

That was probably why she worked harder and more conscientiously than anyone else in the class, as though she had to prove something to herself and to the world, and show everyone that even Lisa Tyler could get the As and the Bs in her test scores, and be up there with the best of them.

Trouble is, thought Lisa, as Jean-Luc continued to regard her with his now-serious eyes, if you crack the joke often enough you'll turn around one day and find that the joke's on you and you've become it!

Jean-Luc smiled at her. "I've played that little trick on every class I have taken here at Applewood," he admitted. "And every single person has fallen for it. But not every person's French is as good as yours . . ."

Lisa looked at the handsome Frenchman in disbelief. "*My* French?" she gasped in amazement, not too sure whether this was another joke Jean-Luc was playing on her. "Come off it now, Jean-Luc! I speak French like Princess Diana understands nuclear physics!"

Jean-Luc laughed at the analogy, but said: "There you are at it again, Lisa. You're putting yourself down!"

Lisa bit her lip. "Sorry," she said, and surprised herself by actually meaning it.

"Your French just needs a little bit of polish and encouragement, that's all," he said.

"They don't have much time for encouragement at Applewood," Lisa said philosophically, warming even more to Jean-Luc. "We're hopelessly understaffed as it is and the teachers spend most of their time trying to come up with schemes to bring more money into the college . . ."

Jean-Luc nodded sympathetically, and leaned down towards Lisa's ear: Lisa suddenly felt very self-conscious as if everyone passing by them in the corridor was watching her. Jean-Luc lowered his voice.

"And anyway," he said in a conspiratorial whisper, "even without encouragement, your French is still much more better than . . . how do you call him – Creepy Crowley!"

Lisa feigned shock. "Jean-Luc! You shouldn't call him that! You're a teacher!"

"Only an *assistant* teacher," he reminded her and his mischievous eyes lit up again. "I know the names you give to all the teachers, Lisa. I often ask myself just what name you give to me . . ."

"Oh, to us you're just Jean-Luc," Lisa said lightly. And also Dreamboat, the Frog's Legs, and French Delight, she added, but only to herself.

"Do you really mean what you said about my French?" she asked, eager both to change the subject and attract more praise her way.

Jean-Luc frowned, as though he was disappointed that Lisa should doubt his word. "Of course I did – I wouldn't have said it otherwise," he said, and grinned.

With those wonderful white teeth, Lisa found herself thinking once again.

"And besides," he continued, "we Frenchmen do not only give compliments just when we are trying to impress pretty young women . . . Sometimes we actually mean them!"

Pretty young women? Now he really is pulling my leg!

"So stop underestimating yourself, Mademoiselle Tyler," he said mock sternly, and wagged a reproving finger in her direction. "You will promise me that, won't you?"

Lisa smiled, and nodded her head. "OK, Jean-Luc, I promise . . ."

"C'est bon!" he said, and looked at his watch, a Swatch so garishly coloured that only a

Frenchman could get away with wearing it. "I have a conversation class with the third year now, and you will be late for your class. *A bientôt, Lisa.*"

"*A bientôt, Jean-Luc,*" said Lisa and fluttered the fingers of her outstretched palm in a gesture of farewell.

As she watched Jean-Luc make his way down the crowded corridor, she felt someone tap her on the back. She turned round to see Chrissie smiling at her.

"Lisa Tyler, talk about a sly one!" she said. "I guess it's true what they say — still waters really do run deep!"

"What do you mean?"

"Now don't tell me that you and French Delight were just talking about work!" Chrissie said accusingly.

Lisa blushed for some unknown reason. "As a matter of fact we were!" she said.

"Oh yeah?" said Chrissie, sounding about as convinced as if someone had just told her that Madonna had joined a convent.

Lisa smiled, privately delighted that Chrissie thought that she might have been trying it on with Jean-Luc, but said: "Let Alison make a fool of herself over Jean-Luc. If he gives me good grades on French Conversation, that's all I'm interested in!"

Chrissie regarded Lisa through narrowed disappointed eyes, and sighed. Lisa was telling the truth after all!

"At least you could help me lay the groundwork for a bit of gossip, Lisa!" she complained.

Lisa shook her head brightly. "Sorry, Chrissie, you're not going to hear any gossip about me and Jean-Luc, so you might as well give up now."

"Shame," said Chrissie with feeling, and looked approvingly at Lisa's white skirt and stylish Chevignon shirt, which made such a contrast to her usual jeans and sloppy sweatshirt. "You look good today, Lisa. If I didn't know you better I'd say you were trying to impress someone . . ."

Lisa laughed at her friend's insatiable appetite for any sort of titillating gossip.

"Now who would I want to impress?" she asked seriously, and headed off towards the Chemistry laboratory. "It's the start of summer, Chrissie, that's all!"

Chrissie nodded her head slowly at the retreating figure of Lisa, not quite certain what to think. There was one thing she was sure of, however. Her nose had begun to twitch, which meant that she was on to something.

Either that, or it was going to rain.

6

When the half-past three bell rang, signalling the end of yet another working day at Applewood, there was usually a mass stampede to get outside the school gates and home to tea and *Neighbours* as soon as possible.

In this respect the teachers were just as bad as the students they taught; very few of them stayed behind to catch up on their administrative work, preferring to do that at home (over tea and *Neighbours*); those that did usually only did because they had to and often resented the extra unpaid hours they put in.

Jean-Luc, however, sauntered casually out of the main school building and across the sunny playground as though he hadn't a care in the world. In the summer sun he could have been taking a stroll down the promenade at Cannes, rather than walking over to his green 2CV parked on the asphalt car park at dreary old Applewood.

Lisa, who was also leaving the school building, envied him his laid-back attitude to life. She supposed it was something to do with him coming from the South of France; there, with the sun shining down for most of the year and the turquoise waves gently lapping the golden beaches, she imagined it must be pretty hard to get wound up about anything. Maybe she ought to try it one day; as long as she caught the train at the correct railway station, that is.

She watched as Jean-Luc was slowly surrounded by a gaggle of giggling second-form girls. He had just started taking this class of twelve-year-olds, and at least half of them had developed major crushes on the Frenchman.

She sniggered as she watched them, gushing over his French accent and dark Mediterranean good looks, and smiled to herself in a superior way.

She'd been just like them at that age, she remembered with a grimace, "falling in love" with all the handsome sixth-formers at the drop of a hat and, along with Chrissie and Alison and all the other girls in her class, making a complete fool of herself in front of any teacher who just happened to be male, reasonably good-looking and under thirty.

Thank God I've got over that now! she thought gratefully.

Jean-Luc's admirers were still hanging around him and chatting inanely, like a bunch of silly teenagers outside the stage door talking to their pop star hero.

49

To Lisa it was an amusing spectacle but it was also clear to her that Jean-Luc was getting more than a little embarrassed at all the unwelcome attention, as he tried to make his way through the throng to his 2CV.

He noticed Lisa watching, and waved to her, urging her to come over and rescue him from his fans. Lisa looked around, and then back at Jean-Luc, as if to say: *Who? Me?*

Jean-Luc laughed, and nodded.

As Lisa crossed the playground, the crowd caught sight of her and dispersed, each one of the girls glaring reproachfully in Lisa's direction. The big girls are moving in now, their meaningful looks seemed to say; there's no chance for us now.

It was a feeling which would have surprised Lisa if she had been aware of it; Lisa had never before considered herself serious competition for anyone (apart from in Chemistry class, of course, where there was no one to beat her in analysing complex polymer chains . . .).

Jean-Luc smiled when Lisa walked up to him. With those wonderfully white teeth.

"*Merci*, Lisa," he sighed with exaggerated relief. "It was getting a little fraught!"

Lisa laughed. "You should feel flattered, Jean-Luc," she said.

Jean-Luc joined in the laughter. "Schoolgirl crushes," he dismissed them. "I'm afraid it comes with the job . . ."

"But all those pretty young girls after you . . ." Lisa said, teasing him as she never would another teacher. After all, she reminded herself, he was only twenty-one.

Jean-Luc stroked his chin thoughtfully and pretended to consider the matter quite seriously for a half-second. Lisa noticed that there were the beginnings of a five o'clock shadow on his face.

Finally he replied: "I think twelve-year-olds are a little too young even for me . . ." He chuckled. "I prefer them a few years older . . ."

He looked at Lisa and, without either of them knowing why, there was suddenly an awkward silence.

Finally Jean-Luc said: "Lisa, you're not wearing your glasses."

Lisa shrugged. "I don't really need them," she explained. "I only use them for reading, but I usually forget to take them off."

"You should take them off more often," Jean-Luc said. "Wearing them all the time is not only bad for your vision, but they also hide your eyes."

"What?"

"They are very beautiful, Lisa," said Jean-Luc and looked down into her baby-blue eyes. "It is a shame to hide them behind your glasses all the time."

Lisa giggled nervously, sounding exactly like one of the twelve-year-olds she had just seen off.

"Jean-Luc, is that a line you're spinning me?" she asked, rather more breezily than she felt.

I do not believe I just said that! she thought immediately after.

Jean-Luc frowned, not quite understanding. "Spinning a line?" he asked.

Lisa raised her eyes heavenwards, realizing that she was rapidly digging a grave for herself right here and now in the school playground. She searched around for the colloquial French expression which Eliane had taught them all the previous term.

"Spinning a line," she repeated, and then remembered. "You know – *faire la drague!*"

"Ah, I see . . ." smiled Jean-Luc, impressed by Lisa's knowledge of French slang. He then took a slightly more serious tone: "Lisa, when I say that a woman's eyes are beautiful I am not 'spinning a line'. I'm simply telling her the truth. And the truth is that your eyes are very beautiful."

Lisa nodded, and contemplated her shoes for a minute, not sure whether she was being complimented further, or being sternly told off by Teacher.

"Yeah, well, OK, I'm sorry," she said to her shoes. She felt Jean-Luc's thumb on her chin and he raised her face to look at him. He was grinning again.

"And besides, I'm French," he said, and winked at her. "We do have a reputation to live up to, you know. If we didn't compliment pretty young women—"

Pretty young women? That's the second time he's used those words to me in as many days!

"—If we didn't compliment pretty young women all the time what would people think of us?" he continued. "They might think that we're as cold and wet and unfeeling as a codfish, or – even worse – as you English!"

Lisa stuck her tongue out at Jean-Luc and raised her arm in a mock attempt to hit him for the slight to her entire country. Jean-Luc stepped back, laughing, and raised his hands in a gesture of surrender.

"OK, I admit defeat," he said. "You win the battle, Lisa!"

"We usually do," she reflected. "Think of Waterloo . . . Think of Agincourt . . ."

"Ah, but we built our part of the Channel Tunnel first," countered Jean-Luc.

"Yes, and you also gave us reflexive verbs, masculine and feminine endings and the past preterite tense."

Jean-Luc's face fell. "That is a disgrace I and my fellow countrymen shall have to live with forever . . . but we did also give the world great writers and philosophers and singers like Edith Piaf," he said, referring to the legendary singer of the fifties and sixties, whose recordings were still loved today in France by both young and old.

"You like Edith Piaf?" asked Lisa in surprise.

"But of course," he replied. "I am French after all . . . but I'm surprised you have even heard of her . . . I would have thought someone your age . . ."

"I'm only four years younger than you, Jean-Luc!" Lisa replied, and explained: "My dad had lots of her songs on CD. Along with our last French assistant that's where I learnt lots of my French slang. I love her songs—"

"Such as?"

Lisa began to sing the words to her favourite French song, the one she always played to herself after she'd seen a particularly sad and romantic movie on TV:

"T'es beau, tu sais,
T'es beau, c'est vrai . . ."

"Why, thank you," said Jean-Luc, and Lisa blushed as she realized the meaning of the French words: "You're handsome, you know, you're handsome, it's true . . ."

"It's good to know that you like Piaf," he continued. "But what about other music?"

Lisa mentioned the Lower Depths, a new indy band who had just broken big in the charts, and whose records everyone in the sixth form seemed to be playing. Jean-Luc had never heard of them, and Lisa urged him to search out one of their cassettes, after he reminded her that he didn't have the money to afford CDs.

Lisa attempted to resume their argument. "And do you agree that the English aren't cold and wet?" she asked.

"Well, not all of them," he admitted reluctantly, and added: "Although some of them pretend all the time that they are . . ."

What does he mean? Lisa asked herself. He can't be talking about me – can he. . . ?

Before she had time to ask, Jean-Luc said: "Look, Lisa, it's getting late—" he gestured around the playground which was now empty – "and you've probably missed your bus."

54

"That's OK," she said. "I've only missed the school bus. I'll get the public bus – you know, the number nine bus – the one that normal people use . . ."

Jean-Luc ignored her and continued: "And as you saved me from the manic lusts of the entire second form just there, the least I can do is offer you a lift home." He pointed to the green 2CV.

"Jean-Luc, you don't have to—" Lisa began but the Frenchman put a silencing finger to her lips.

"I insist," he said. "That is, if you can bear to be seen with me in a *deux chevaux*. I know what the English think of these cars . . ."

"That they're clapped-out pieces of junk only driven by left-wing vegetarian feminists wearing badges banning the bomb and supporting the whales?" Lisa asked with a daring twinkle in her eye.

Jean-Luc burst out laughing again. "Well, something like that," he agreed, and regarded Lisa with renewed interest.

Not only was she pretty in a curious sort of way, but she was also very intelligent, and, when she let herself go, extraordinarily funny. It was a long time since Jean-Luc had laughed with a girl roughly his own age. More often than not when girls came up and introduced themselves to him it was with only one thing in mind; Lisa made a welcome and refreshing change.

"They are also very cheap," he reminded her, returning to the subject of the 2CV. "And for a poor student like me – even if I am your teacher – that is the most important thing. It is also fast, stylish, unpredictable and totally unique – just like we French!"

Lisa decided that there was only one thing in the world she would prefer to be doing right now; and, as the latest teenage heart-throbs were probably busy somewhere making a video or advertising underwear, she would have to settle for being driven home by Jean-Luc in his 2CV.

They began to walk towards the car when a voice called out from behind them: "Jean-Luc! Jean-Luc, wait!"

Both of them turned around to see Alison running towards them. Today she was wearing a chic leather jacket and a green Lycra work-out suit.

"Bonjour, Alison," said Jean-Luc pleasantly as Alison came up to them. Lisa just stared suspiciously at the other girl; she'd known her classmate long enough now to know that she was up to something.

Alison nodded briefly at Lisa, as if to acknowledge her presence, and then devoted all her considerable attentions to Jean-Luc.

"Am I glad I caught up with you," she said, panting for breath.

Jean-Luc was instantly concerned. "Why? What is the matter?" he asked.

She looked up beseechingly at Jean-Luc while Lisa just continued to glare at her rival.

"Well, it's just that I stayed behind in the library reading up on my French homework . . ." Alison began, and flicked back her gorgeous long red hair.

Oh yeah? thought Lisa ungraciously. The last

time you were in a library anywhere was when you fancied the hunky young librarian in the public library!

However, by her side Jean-Luc seemed to be impressed; although whether it was by the fact that Alison had been pursuing her studies so assiduously, or by her Lycra work-out suit, Lisa couldn't be quite sure.

"And the next thing I know—" Alison looked at her watch – an expensive one which her father had given her last year as a sixteenth-birthday present – "it's a quarter to four and I've missed the bus home..." She fluttered her eyelids seductively up at Jean-Luc.

"There's always the number nine," Lisa reminded her coldly.

Alison shot an evil look in Lisa's direction before continuing.

"Of course I would get the number nine, but it takes me *soooo* much out of my way – and I do have an aerobics class at the leisure centre tonight which I really don't want to be late for – I do think we should be as fit as we can be, don't you, Jean-Luc? – and I was wondering if..."

Jean-Luc got the hint and smiled. "Well, I was just offering Lisa a lift home," he said. "There's always room for one more..."

Jean-Luc, how can you be so stupid? Lisa thought.

"Jean-Luc, Alison lives miles away from me," she said, and instantly regretted saying it.

"Oh that's all right," Alison said sweetly. "Jean-Luc can drop you off first and then take me home, can't you, Jean-Luc?"

"Well, er . . . I suppose so . . ."

And you really went and asked for that one now, didn't you, Lisa?

Vaguely aware that something was not quite right, Jean-Luc looked at Lisa, who was gritting her teeth and glaring malevolently at Alison. Alison reciprocated by flashing Lisa a triumphant look.

Jean-Luc shrugged his shoulders philosophically, deciding that, like all Frenchmen before him, he would never really understand the female of the species, no matter how hard he tried.

"Well, shall we go?" he asked brightly.

"Why not?" said Lisa in a dark monotone, so frosty that it could have frozen water.

Alison skipped over to Jean-Luc's green 2CV, and stood by the passenger door, which Jean-Luc opened for her.

"Why, *merci, monsieur*," she cooed, and bent down to enter the car, at the same time making sure that the Frenchman had a good look at her almost-perfect figure.

Jean-Luc smiled at Alison's far-from-subtle flirtatiousness. *"Je vous en prie, mademoiselle,"* he chuckled.

This just makes me so sick! Lisa fumed to herself as she found herself meekly accepting the back seat of the 2CV, while Jean-Luc sat in the driver's seat, next to Alison, who was already resting a leisurely and familiar arm around the back of his seat. Why does Alison have to go and spoil everything?

Spoil everything? This is just a lift home from

my teacher, isn't it?

And suddenly Lisa realized that, for her, Jean-Luc was something more — something much, much more — than just a mere teacher.

7

"Well, here comes the teacher's pet," sneered Simon the following day as Alison strode into the common room with a self-satisfied look on her face.

At his side, Lisa looked up urgently from her French novel. "What d'you mean?" she asked.

"She and the new French assistant, they're like that," said Si and crossed his fingers.

Chrissie, who was also sitting with them, suddenly became interested. If this was gossip then she decided that she ought to hear about it. She urged Si to continue.

"I only saw her last night in Jean-Luc's car," Si said. "Looking very friendly together, if you ask me . . ."

"That's nothing," said Lisa quickly. "He gave me a lift home too last night . . ."

"Well," said Si, who had caught the urgency in Lisa's voice. "It seemed considerably more than just a lift home to me . . ."

"Maybe they're having an affair!" Chrissie suggested gleefully, oblivious to Lisa's feelings, and already looking forward to spreading the gossip around. She looked at Simon with new interest: when he wasn't pretending to be Elvis Presley he loved gossip almost as much as she did! Maybe he was normal after all!

She sighed. "Alison's a lucky so-and-so. But I suppose it was inevitable: the handsome swarthy hunk from the Mediterranean and the pale-skinned, red-headed temptress from the lower sixth. Typical Barbara Cartland material, really. We should all have seen it coming!"

Lisa stood up angrily, knocking her book to the floor, which she refused to pick up. "Just because Jean-Luc gives her a lift home you automatically think that they're going out together! Men and women can get on very well together without having a raging affair, you know!"

Si flinched at Lisa's outburst. "Hey, I'm sorry if I stepped on somebody's toes . . ." he said.

"It's nothing," Lisa lied.

Chrissie stood up and took Lisa's arm. "Of course it's nothing," she said, and led Lisa away. As soon as they were out of Si's earshot she said: "OK Lisa, what's the matter?"

Lisa shrugged. "It's nothing," she repeated. "But I wish people wouldn't jump to conclusions . . . and anyway, Jean-Luc drove me home last night as well. Who's to say he's not going out with me?"

Chrissie nodded wisely, and looked over to Alison who, as usual, was surrounded by an

61

entourage of friends and hangers-on. Lisa wouldn't be the first girl in the sixth form to be envious of Alison's outgoing personality and lifestyle.

"Well, it's just that Alison has a . . . well, let's say a bit of a reputation for getting the boys," she said tactfully. "And she and Jean-Luc would make a very good-looking pair, you've got to admit that . . ."

"Meaning I wouldn't, I suppose?" Lisa snapped back.

"Of course I didn't mean that," Chrissie insisted. "You're as attractive as they come, Lisa . . ." Her voice tailed off.

"But?" demanded Lisa.

"But lighten up a little, Lisa. Life isn't all work, you know. Sometimes you're so serious you frighten people off . . ." Chrissie avoided Lisa's eyes as she added: "And do something about your hair . . ."

"My hair?" Lisa asked and flicked back her pony-tail.

"Pony-tails belong in the fourth form," Chrissie said.

"But it's practical," Lisa said. "It keeps my hair out of my eyes during Chemistry and Biology . . ."

Chrissie smiled kindly at her friend. "This is Life in the Sixth Form, Lisa," she announced grandly. "It's not supposed to be practical!"

Lisa grinned in spite of herself, and looked over at Alison once more. "Do you really think they're going out together?"

"Who?" asked Chrissie, who had already forgotten the original topic of conversation.

"Alison and Jean-Luc."

Chrissie shrugged.

"She'd certainly like to," she admitted. "But I really don't have a clue. Still, it's a good story to spread around, isn't it?"

Lisa gave Chrissie a look which plainly said: No, it isn't.

"Anyway, why all this interest in Jean-Luc's love life all of a sudden?" asked Chrissie, although she suspected she already knew the answer, even if Lisa didn't know herself.

"Just curious, that's all," said Lisa rather feebly. Chrissie was about to follow up on her line of questioning when Alison left her tiny group and swanned over to them.

"Well, *bonjour mes amies*," she cooed with an over-the-top French accent.

"You look like the cat who's got the cream," Chrissie remarked.

Alison looked meaningfully over at Lisa. "No, just a chauffeur," she said wickedly. "Jean-Luc was *soooo* nice to me last night, driving me home, and then to my aerobics class . . ."

"He took you to the leisure centre as well?" marvelled Chrissie while, beside her, Lisa just glared at Alison.

"Of course," Alison said, as though it was the most natural thing in the world for a teacher to drive her home, wait while she collected her sportsgear, and then chauffeur her to the sports centre. "He is *such* a gentleman . . ."

Chrissie imagined, rightly, that Jean-Luc would have had little say in the matter. Alison would have browbeaten him to drive her, especially as the leisure centre was probably on his way home. Indeed it was notoriously difficult to resist Alison when she had set her mind on something.

"Well, *au revoir*, girls, Jean-Luc and I'll see you in French later," Alison said cheerily, satisfied that she had ensured that Lisa knew of her minor triumph. She waltzed out of the common room.

"You can't help admiring her cheek, can you, Lisa?" asked Chrissie, clearly impressed by Alison's coup.

"So he gave her a lift home? So he gave her a lift to the leisure centre? So what?" said Lisa through gritted teeth. "It doesn't mean anything, does it? It doesn't matter."

But Lisa knew that it mattered quite a lot.

For the rest of the day the atmosphere between Lisa and Alison was, to say the least, glacial. The bad feeling finally came to a head in the French lesson, the last class of the afternoon.

Both Mr Crowley and Jean-Luc were taking the class, with Alison once more at the front of the class, openly flirting with the Frenchman, who seemed quite embarrassed by all the attention she was giving him. It was obvious that the news of the lift home had spread all around the class by now, and everyone had drawn the conclusion Alison had wanted them to draw.

Lisa, meanwhile, sat moodily at the back of the classroom, idly looking out of the window and stubbornly refusing to answer Jean-Luc's questions when he addressed her.

This is silly and childish, she reminded herself but continued to do it; so what if Jean-Luc fancies Alison? It's not as if I ever had a chance with him.

But does she have to make it so blasted obvious?

Finally it was half-past three and school was over for the day. As everyone began to bustle out of the classroom Crowley called Lisa over to his desk.

Alison paraded past the desk behind which Jean-Luc was also sitting.

"Au revoir, Jean-Luc," she cooed.

"Good afternoon, Alison," he replied. Lisa noted that the Frenchman was grinning with amusement, and also that he had pointedly replied to Alison in English.

Lisa took a deep breath, sure that Crowley was going to reprimand her for her uncooperative behaviour in class today. Instead he harrumphed and smiled at her.

"I've been looking at your work, Miss Tyler, and it's quite promising," he began, although in truth he had done nothing of the kind; it was Jean-Luc who had drawn Lisa's work to his attention. "You seem to have quite a talent for languages."

"Thank you," said Lisa, surprised at this unaccustomed piece of praise from Creepy Crowley who usually had trouble remembering people's names, let alone their test scores.

"Your grades are good," he said, looking down at the class register on to which he entered the students' marks for their essays and class-work. "But I feel—" he looked at Jean-Luc — "*we* feel that with a little bit of extra work they could be even better . . ."

Oh great, thought Lisa, he's going to give me extra homework!

"What we are proposing – if, of course, you are agreeable, Miss Tyler – is some extra lunchtime tuition in French conversation."

"All free of charge of course," said Jean-Luc and looked up and smiled at her.

With that gorgeous smile.

Crowley glanced curiously at Jean-Luc but didn't say anything.

Vitally aware of Jean-Luc's presence, Lisa still continued to look at Crowley.

"With you, sir?" she asked.

"No, with *me*," interrupted Jean-Luc. "As I told you before, Lisa, all you need is a little more encouragement and practice and you could even be university material."

Lisa looked at Jean-Luc with mixed feelings, wondering how much truth there was in Alison's unspoken claim – that she and Jean-Luc were practically going out together – and then wondered how she would feel working side by side with the handsome young Frenchman with the brilliantly white teeth who smelt of soap and roses and starched white shirts.

Who am I kidding to think that he's got any interest in me? Someone as cute as Jean-Luc could have any girl he wants. And how am I going to feel working alongside him, and knowing that he's going out with Alison? I'd feel frustrated, I'd feel like a fool!

Lisa took a deep breath, and looked Crowley directly in the eyes. "No," she said. "It's a very kind offer, but no thank you."

Crowley briefly raised an eyebrow in surprise and then began to gather up his papers.

"Very well, Miss Tyler, if that is your decision . . ." He stood up and left the classroom.

"Lisa, why did you say no?" asked Jean-Luc. There was a disappointed expression on his face.

Lisa shrugged. "I've too much work already, Jean-Luc," she said coldly, "and I'm sure there are better things you could be doing than talking in French to me during your lunch break."

"I don't understand you at all, Lisa," he said, clearly mystified, "but if you change your mind the offer's still open . . ."

He looked at his Swatch. "It's late and I've made you miss your bus home again," he remarked. "Can I drive you home?"

"Thanks, Jean-Luc, but no thanks," Lisa said frostily. "I'll catch the bus." And with that she walked out of the classroom.

Jean-Luc stared after her, and ran his fingers through his thick black hair in desperation. What is wrong with that girl? he asked himself.

And why am I so concerned that she isn't going to study with me?

"Lisa Tyler, you are the most idiotic, senseless, brain-dead thing since fishes crawled out of the ocean and up on to dry land," Chrissie's voice crackled angrily down the telephone line later that evening.

Chrissie had rung Lisa up to ask for advice on some homework and instead had heard the craziest story since Alison Potter had said she was going to give up men for Lent.

"No, I'm not," countered Lisa. "I really don't have the time for extra French lessons. And it was you, after all, Chrissie, who said that life shouldn't be all work, wasn't it?"

"Well, yes, but this is different . . ."

"And just *how* is it different?"

"Lisa, we are talking here about French Delight, the most gorgeous, sexiest, hunkiest guy that ever walked the face of this Earth – well, Applewood anyway – besides that, he's foreign. There are girls in the fifth form who would sell their mothers to have private lessons with him. And what do you do, Lisa Tyler? You say no!"

"You think I did the wrong thing?"

"Too right you did the wrong thing!"

"Chrissie, I'm not interested in how sexy or handsome Jean-Luc is," Lisa claimed.

Oh yeah? Chrissie thought.

"But I haven't got the time . . ." Lisa continued.

Who am I fooling? Lisa thought. My social calendar is about as exciting as a wet Wednesday in Margate. And Chrissie is right: Jean-Luc is very sexy.

"Look, Lisa," Chrissie said, and her voice took on a serious tone. "You're good at French, right?"

"Right."

"Well, if you accept Jean-Luc's offer you'll be even better." She laughed ironically. "Forget how gorgeous he is. Forget that two-thirds of the female population of Applewood happen to worship the very ground that he walks on. Forget that Alison Potter would kill to be in your shoes—"

"Alison?" Lisa asked urgently. "What's she got to do with it?"

"Well, you didn't believe that rubbish about her and Jean-Luc, now, did you?" asked Chrissie.

Actually I did, thought Lisa. "Of course not," she said.

"Alison's all talk," said Chrissie. "Grow up, Lisa! OK, she's the best-looking of us all, and a hit with boys her own age – but with someone four years older than her? And a teacher? And French? It's going to take a lot more than her wiggling and fluttering her eyelids for her to get Jean-Luc—"

"You really think so?" asked Lisa eagerly, and quickly corrected herself. "I mean, what's that got to do with me?"

Chrissie laughed down the phone line. "Come off it, Lisa! I've seen how you react when Jean-Luc's around . . ."

"What do you mean?" asked Lisa.

"The minute he gets anywhere near you, you tense up . . ."

"I don't," Lisa snapped back defensively.

"I'm your best friend, Lisa, and I know you do," pressed Chrissie. "And in my book that means one of two things. Either you can't stand the sight of him—"

"Or?"

"Well, what do you think?" asked Chrissie and chuckled. "Good luck to you, is what I say. If he was offering me French lessons I'd take them like a shot!"

At the other end of the telephone line Lisa found herself going red with embarrassment. She laughed nervously down the phone.

"And what chance would I have with him?" she asked Chrissie, realizing that what she was hoping for was a positive answer.

"As much as any of us," came the rather disappointing reply. "But get serious, Lisa—"

"You're the one always telling me not to be," Lisa interrupted.

"Go to the lessons," she urged and added sneakily: "If not for French Delight, then for the grades."

"You really think I should?"

"Of course, you idiot . . . and if you get on well with French Delight, then who knows. . . ?"

So Lisa resolved to accept Jean-Luc's offer of free French lessons. She also resolved to keep the lessons strictly on a business-level.

On the other end of the line, Chrissie laughed silently to herself. She'd like to see anyone keep anything on a business-level with Jean-Luc Roupie!

8

Lisa felt awkward as she sat next to Jean-Luc the next day, poring over a copy of *Paris-Match*, the weekly French news magazine to which the school subscribed. It wasn't just the fact that, as it was a particularly hot day, Jean-Luc had come to school dressed in blue jeans and a white T-shirt which showed off his tan and also proved – as Alison had correctly guessed – that he really did have muscles.

Her conversation with Chrissie on the phone the previous night had hit a raw nerve. Lisa finally had to admit that she was attracted to Jean-Luc. It wasn't just his good looks, although one would have to be blind not to have been struck by them.

Lisa liked the mischievous twinkle in his eyes when he played a joke on his classes; and when his jokes backfired – as had the one about the railway station – the genuine look of concern on his face.

She loved his accent and his inimitable *Frenchness*, the way that no matter what he was wearing, whether it was today's T-shirt, or a collar and tie (when he wanted to impress the principal) he wore it with style and elegance.

And she adored the way in which he encouraged her in her studies, so unlike Creepy Crowley, and always sought to boost her confidence.

But she wondered whether this was a genuine fondness for the Frenchman, or just a silly schoolgirl crush. Probably the latter, she scolded herself, and I'm a little too old for that now! What signs has he shown that he's even interested in me? Calling me a pretty young woman is hardly a sign of eternal devotion, now, is it? she reasoned.

Whichever it was, she decided that it was a ridiculous concept. After all, apart from the fact that he was a member of the teaching staff he was twenty-one, four years older than her. He'd probably had lots of girlfriends in the past, if the things people said about Frenchmen were even halfway true. And Lisa had never had a serious boyfriend before; that is, if you didn't count last Christmas's kiss under the mistletoe with James.

More to the point, Jean-Luc was quite simply gorgeous, impossibly so. And that, for some peculiar reason, made Lisa feel even more uncomfortable. He was so gorgeous in fact that Lisa bet that he frightened a lot of people off.

She remembered something the undoubtedly very attractive Alison had once said to her and Chrissie during one of her particularly catty and superior moods: "I really wish I was plain! Boys get scared off when you're so good-looking. They're frightened that if they try and chat you up you'll just turn around and tell them where to get off. That's why I seem to do all the running after them!"

Well, Lisa determined that she at least wasn't going to do the running after Jean-Luc. Theirs was going to be a strictly teacher-pupil relationship.

And unlike half of the other girls in the sixth form, she decided, I'm going to ignore his good looks, his hairy muscular arms, that boyish way he licks his lips before he starts to address the class, his cute little smile . . .

Jean-Luc looked up from the copy of the magazine and smiled: "I'm glad you changed your mind, Lisa," he said in English.

Lisa muttered her acknowledgement and returned to reading out aloud in French from the magazine.

"I'm also glad that you've taken your hair out of its pony-tail," he continued. "It makes your face look much more softer."

Lisa looked up to find herself staring right into Jean-Luc's eyes. She coloured.

"Thanks very much, Jean-Luc," she said a little coolly. "Now can we just carry on with the lesson, please?"

Jean-Luc frowned; why was Lisa being so frosty with him? He was merely complimenting her. And it was true, now that she had let her hair down, her face did look much less severe. Although he wondered why he never noticed when any other of his female students changed their hairstyles.

They turned over the page of the magazine, to an article on Cannes, Jean-Luc's home town.

"It must be wonderful living there," Lisa said, in her acceptable French, the pronunciation of which Jean-Luc would occasionally correct. "Sunshine all day, the sea on your back doorstep, taking life as it comes . . ."

Jean-Luc laughed. "It would be even better without the tourists," he said. "In August all of France seems to come down to the Riviera. You cannot move for Parisians, and the beaches are littered with cans and rubbish and pale white bodies, and the air is full of car exhaust fumes . . ."

"What do you expect when you drive a 2CV?" Lisa asked fliply, as Jean-Luc moved over to the bookshelf where he took down a map of France and opened it on the table in front of them.

He pointed to a small town on the outskirts of Cannes. "That is La Napoule," he said in French, "where my mother lives, and where I was born. Many yachts go there, and millionaires often eat in the town."

"You make it sound very glamorous," said Lisa. "Don't you miss it?"

Jean-Luc switched back to English. "Sometimes, when the English summer starts raining dogs and cats—"

"Cats and dogs," Lisa corrected him patiently, but couldn't help smiling. Jean-Luc grinned.

"But there are compensations to living in England," he continued. "On the Riviera people are so superficial. They are concerned only about appearances, about how people look, and not how they *are*. All they worry about is their money or their tan or buying the latest designer clothing . . . I prefer things much more simpler . . ."

"Simpler," Lisa corrected him again, and when Jean-Luc frowned, not understanding, she explained: "It's 'simpler', or 'more simple', not 'more simpler' . . . You're always getting that wrong, Jean-Luc!"

Jean-Luc raised his hands in an affected gesture of saddened defeat. "So, the pupil becomes the teacher!" he said.

"Sorry," said Lisa automatically.

"There's no need to be sorry," he said and laid a hand on her arm, before Lisa quickly moved it away. "If I say something wrong you must correct me, that's the only way to learn. Otherwise I will be convinced that people are laughing at my mistakes behind my back. And I'm sure there's a lot you could teach me, Lisa."

Is he coming on to me or what? Lisa asked herself urgently, not quite sure what to think. Or am I reading too much into this?

"Well, I'd much rather sit on the promenade at Cannes every day than be stuck in boring old Applewood," she said, deftly changing the subject.

"La Croisette," said Jean-Luc.

"What?"

"La Croisette," he repeated, and continued in French: "That is the name of the boulevard in Cannes which stretches along the seafront. It's very famous for its restaurants and nightlife . . ."

75

"I can just imagine you in Cannes now," said Lisa in French, "dining off pâté de foie gras in an expensive restaurant, with a glass of Pernod at your side, in the company of an absolutely breathtaking girlfriend."

Jean-Luc laughed. "I'm sorry to shatter your illusions, Lisa," he said with a grin. "We're not all millionaires on the Côte d'Azur, you know. My favourite restaurant on the Croisette is a low-price pizzeria which is always packed, I hardly ever drink alcohol — and I don't have a girlfriend — either in Cannes or here in England."

"Hey, I didn't mean to pry," Lisa said quickly in English, as she suddenly felt her heart leap for joy. She reverted to French: "Your private life's your own concern."

"I didn't think you were prying," claimed Jean-Luc, with a twinkle in his eye. "After all, why should you pry? You're not a gossip like Chrissie—"

"Oh, Chrissie's harmless enough," Lisa defended her friend. "She likes a good story, that's all."

"Nor do you have a personal concern, like Alison . . ."

"Alison?" asked Lisa, and wondered why it was that she could say things in a foreign language like French which she would never dream of saying in English. "But I thought that you two got on really well . . ."

Jean-Luc grinned. "She'd like us to, I know that," he admitted. "But I'm not interested in her at all. She's too pushy, too forward. When it comes right down to it she isn't really very interesting at all. People who go about flaunting themselves are usually very superficial: I'm not interested in them, no matter how attractive they might be. I'm not concerned with how people look, Lisa; it's what they are that really matters . . ."

He seemed to consider the matter for a moment before adding wickedly: 'Of course, if they're intelligent, cultured and look like Beatrice Dalle I'm hardly going to say no, now am I?"

Lisa giggled. "You know that Alison's going around saying that you are two are like that—" she crossed her fingers in an imitation of Simon's earlier gesture.

"How childish," he said, and sighed: "Still, I suppose she'll never stop trying."

"We all say Alison's like the Mounties," Lisa said. "She always gets her man!"

Jean-Luc shook his head. "But not this man, Lisa," he said, and looked at her strangely. "Alison will not get *this* man!"

He turned his attention back to the magazine. "And now, Lisa, shall we get back down to work?"

Lisa nodded her head, and resumed her reading. As Jean-Luc turned the pages of *Paris-Match* his bare arm accidentally brushed against the skin of hers. A frisson of delight shot through her.

Suddenly Lisa found it very difficult to concentrate on her work. Indeed, work was now the last thing on her mind.

9

Chrissie groaned and lifted her arms heavenwards in desperation. "Why did I ever let
myself get talked into this?" she asked no one in
particular.

Standing by her side Lisa tutted good-naturedly.
"You volunteered to be on the organizing com-
mittee of the summer ball, Chrissie," she reminded her. "No one forced you."

For the sixth form the summer ball was the big
social event of the year; even though it was in
part financed by the school, and in part from
ticket sales, it had the great attraction of being
organized mainly by the students themselves
with the minimum of adult supervision. Even
on the night of the ball, held in the college's
assembly hall, there would only be a few teachers
present, to check that things weren't getting too
out of hand.

Chrissie looked up from the mountain of paperwork before her on a table in the school library.

It seemed that every lunchtime for the past three weeks she'd brought the same mound of papers into the library and the pile never seemed to go down.

"But I never imagined it would be so much hard work — I've got to arrange to have tickets printed; I've got to hire a DJ—"

"Try Si," Lisa suggested mischievously. "He's got a great record collection."

"Lisa, grow up!" Chrissie laughed. "Simon still thinks he's living in a late nineteen-fifties movie. This is the nineties, Lisa. We need up-to-date sounds, not crackly old vinyl passed down to him from his dad! I saw his record collection the other day . . ."

"Oh?"

Chrissie flushed. "I . . . er, I had to get a text book off him so I went round to his house . . ." She changed the subject, indicating the pile of paperwork before her, and looked appealingly at Lisa. "C'mon, Lisa, you're my best friend," she pleaded desperately. "Can't you help me?"

Lisa shook her head sadly; much as she would have liked to have helped in setting up the summer ball there were more important matters to attend to at the moment.

"Sorry," she said, meaning it, "but remember I've got French lessons at lunchtime now."

Chrissie looked curiously at Lisa. The original arrangement with Jean-Luc five weeks ago had been for one lesson a week; now that number had increased to three a week.

Chrissie adopted a superior expression and

stared down her nose at Lisa, something which was particularly difficult to do as Lisa was standing and she was seated at the table.

"I think we've all of us by now got a pretty good idea what you two get up to in your 'French' lessons," she said snidely, although not maliciously.

Lisa pretended to be shocked. Secretly she was delighted by the suspicion that her and Jean-Luc's meetings were not as educational as in fact they were.

"Chrissie!"

"Well, is he giving anyone else private French lessons?" Chrissie asked pertinently.

"As a matter of fact, yes," revealed Lisa. "Stuart Richardson's having a private lesson one hour a week after school . . ."

"Aha!" cried Chrissie, spotting the flaw in Lisa's argument. "But Stuart's dad's paying for that, so at least Jean-Luc's making some money out of it. Yours are free lessons, when Jean-Luc could be charging others for the lessons!"

Lisa blushed: she seemed to be doing a lot of that lately, at least whenever Jean-Luc's name came up.

"Chrissie, we're just good friends," she insisted.

"Of course you are, Lisa . . ."

"He's my teacher; and if we were more than 'just good friends' his job would probably be on the line," Lisa pointed out. "And I know how you like dishing the dirt, so don't you dare go spreading any gossip around," she added, half-hoping that she would.

"So if you don't – you know – what *do* you get up to in your 'French' lessons then?" Chrissie wanted to know.

"We discuss articles in French magazines, sometimes talk about French politics and cinema . . ."

Chrissie grimaced. "He's too cute to talk about serious and intelligent things like that!" she groaned, and shook her head dramatically. "It doesn't seem right somehow!"

"Well, that just shows how wrong you are, judging people solely by appearances," Lisa said smugly; and continued: "Sometimes we talk about life in the South of France and his home town—"

This sounded more interesting. "Any more like him back home?" Chrissie demanded urgently.

Lisa shook her head. "Only son, of a widowed mother," she offered.

"Girlfriend?"

Lisa shook her head again.

"Rich? Prospects?"

Lisa burst out laughing. "Chrissie, what is this? A questionnaire?"

"Well, we girls have to be choosy these days, you know, Lisa. You can't be too careful . . ."

Chrissie continued in a more serious vein. "Whatever he is, he's certainly made a change in you."

"What d'you mean?"

"Your French grades have gone up for one thing."

"And?"

"You're wearing your hair long now – it suits you," Chrissie said.

Lisa ran her fingers self-consciously through her long blonde hair. "Well, you did say it would soften my appearance and look more attractive—"

"Yes, I did, didn't I?" said Chrissie, understanding everything.

Not only that, but Chrissie noted that Lisa was remembering to take off her glasses when she wasn't reading, and had started taking more care in the clothes she wore to school every day.

Lisa could hardly ever have been called scruffy, and had always taken a pride in her appearance; but now she dressed less and less in her baggy sweatshirts and had taken to wearing freshly laundered blouses and T-shirts, and, as the weather improved, bright summer dresses. There was a new bounce in her step, and as she walked along the corridors of Applewood College boys who had known her for six or seven years were beginning to take notice of her.

Lisa attempted to change the subject, and gestured towards Chrissie's pile of paperwork.

"So when is the summer ball?" she asked her.

"The week before the final week of term. It's going to be fun — the upper sixth are going to try and sneak some wine in. Are you going to come?"

Lisa hesitated. "Go on, Lisa," urged Chrissie and added wickedly: "You could invite French Delight . . ." Lisa took a friendly swipe at her friend.

"Or James," she suggested. "He'll be down from university for the holidays . . ."

Lisa made a face. "Ugh, train-spotter James? What a terrible thought . . ."

As they burst out laughing (rather guiltily, it must be said, on Lisa's part at least), Alison entered the library and marched over to Chrissie's table. She eyed the mountain of paperwork curiously until Chrissie explained it was all for the summer ball.

"Put me down for two tickets then," she told Chrissie.

Lisa, in a friendly manner, asked: "So who will you be going with?"

Alison shrugged, and looked at Lisa, pretending to notice her for the first time.

"Oh, I haven't decided yet," she said airily. "There are so many boys who'd like to go with me, you know . . . And who are you going with, Lisa?"

"I don't know yet," she admitted and Alison tutted sympathetically.

"Well, if you can't get a date, Lisa, just let me know," she said. "I'm sure one of the boys I turn down might be persuaded to accompany you . . ."

And with that Alison swished out of the library, which wasn't a place she frequented at the best of times.

Lisa stood there speechless, while Chrissie chuckled.

"I don't believe it!" Lisa finally said. "As if I'd want to go out with one of her cast-offs!"

With Alison's reputation, half the boys in the upper sixth are her cast-offs! Chrissie thought.

"Why is she being like that to me, Chrissie?" she demanded. "We've never really been friends before, but I've done nothing to upset her. What reason does she have for being so catty to me now?"

"Isn't it obvious?" asked Chrissie. "She can't wait to get her hands on French Delight . . . And is he responding? No way . . ."

"But how can any normal red-blooded Frenchman not respond to Alison?" asked Lisa in disbelief. "She's the most glamorous and sophisticated one of us all. She could have any boy she wanted. The only straight boy who hasn't come on to Alison so far is Stuart, and that's only because Helen would murder him if he did."

"What was it you just told me about never judging by appearances, Lisa?" said Chrissie. "Maybe French Delight doesn't like women to throw themselves at him . . . Maybe he prefers women to be more lady-like, and not like a she-devil on heat . . ."

"He did say that he thought she was too childish."

"Did he now?" asked Chrissie and wondered what else Jean-Luc had told her best friend during their private lessons together.

"But why should that turn her against me?" asked Lisa.

"Alison isn't used to losing," explained Chrissie. "And, as far as she's concerned, in the French Delight stakes, you're winning—"

"But we're—"

"I know – 'just good friends'," Chrissie finished for her although her tone suggested that she clearly didn't believe it. "But that's not how *she's* seeing it." And with Alison's experience she should know!

"But she's wrong . . ." I think . . .

"Watch out for Alison, Lisa," Chrissie warned her as she returned to her paperwork. "What Alison wants she'll stop at nothing to get. Don't make an enemy out of her, Lisa, or you'll regret it . . ."

Later that night Lisa and her mother, Maddy, were sitting in front of the television watching a particularly weepy movie. Maddy relished these occasions, which were becoming all too rare as Lisa studied more and more for her exams.

She liked to spend as much time with her daughter as possible; now that Lisa was growing up their relationship was becoming much more one of two good girlfriends rather than that of a mother and daughter.

The movie ended and Maddy switched over channels with the remote control. She dabbed at her eyes with a tissue: these old black-and-white films always made her cry.

Curled up on the sofa, Lisa laughed at her mother's sentimentality: Maddy stuck a not-too-motherly tongue out at her daughter.

"So you've got a softie for your mother," Maddy said. "Those old love stories always get me right there . . ."

Lisa paused and then looked up at her mother before asking: "Mum, how did you know you were in love with Dad?"

Maddy looked strangely at her daughter. "What's brought this on?" she quizzed her.

Lisa shrugged. "Just watching that old film,

I suppose," she said, hoping that she sounded convincing enough. "But how did you know that you were in love with Dad?"

Maddy half-smiled and stared into space, remembering her husband who had died six years ago, and the time when she had first bumped into him almost twenty years ago in the student union bar in her final year at college.

"I was the last one to know," she recalled. "Everyone else seemed to know we were going to be together even before we did.

"I started enjoying his company, looking forward to seeing him every day. I began to feel totally at ease with him . . ."

"Well, I enjoy James's company, and we get on really great together, but I'm hardly in love with him," said Lisa, remembering once more that Christmas kiss under the mistletoe.

"Let me finish," said her mother, who was clearly enjoying her reminiscences. "And then you find yourself laughing at exactly the same things, and sharing the same interests. Finding that that book you read last year he's reading today; or discovering that you both have the same tastes in music, or painting, or movies."

"I thought people always said that opposites attract?" said Lisa.

"Well, sometimes they do," admitted Maddy. "And when you find that there are certain interests you don't share, then you go out and try to find out as much as you can about that subject — because it's what interests *him*.

"And then you start wanting to know everything

about that other person . . . where he comes from, what he likes to eat, the sort of music he likes . . ."

"You make it sound like the third degree!" joked Lisa.

Maddy smiled, and continued: "And suddenly there comes a moment when you realize that there's not a single day that doesn't go by when you don't think of him. That you can't even brush against his skin without shivering all over." She glanced knowingly over at Lisa, who was taking in her every word.

"Sometimes you try and convince yourself that it's not love at all, that it's wishful thinking on your part; that someone as wonderful as he is simply couldn't be falling in love with someone as ordinary as you . . ."

I'm not ordinary! thought Lisa, even though she realized – or hoped – that Maddy wasn't talking about her.

"But deep, deep down inside, you really know," Maddy concluded. "You really know that this is the person you want to spend the whole rest of your life with. You might not be lovers yet, you might not even have kissed each other, but something inside you tells you that this is the one."

"But what is it?" asked Lisa. "What is it that tells you?"

Maddy chuckled. "I don't know. Some unlucky people never have that feeling, some people only experience it late in life. I was fortunate that I met your father when I did . . ." She sighed, not with sorrow but with fondness. "I still miss him, you know, Lisa."

"So do I . . ." agreed her daughter. "Do you think you'll ever marry again?"

Maddy shook her head. "No," she said resolutely. "You see, Lisa, I think that in your life there is one person, and one person only, who is absolutely right for you. Your soulmate, if you like.

"Some people never meet their soulmate, but if you do, you know instinctively that he's the right one for you, and you'd do anything for him. Follow him to the ends of the earth if needs be." She chuckled again. "At least that's how I felt about your poor father – still do, as a matter of fact."

"You must have loved him a lot," said Lisa.

"I did, and always will," said Maddy, and changed the subject slightly. "Are you going to pursue this line of questioning every time we watch an old black-and-white weepie together?"

"No . . ." Lisa smiled.

"You shouldn't really be up this late with school tomorrow," Maddy reproved and glanced at the digital display on the video recorder which read 01.15. She stood up to go to the kitchen to make her customary final cup of cocoa before turning in for the night.

"I was having a word with Miss Greenwood the other day," she said, referring to Lisa's appropriately-named Biology teacher. "She told me that you're not paying enough attention in class these days . . ."

"Oh Mum!" said Lisa, pretending not to feel concerned. "Greenie's finished with the interesting stuff like reproduction and human biology!

Now we're on to boring things like plants and frogs!"

"She said your grades were slipping," her mother continued. "In Chemistry as well, she says."

Lisa averted her eyes from her mother; it was true: in the past few weeks she had indeed received two B-minuses and one C. It was hardly a disaster but, given Lisa's previous track record, it did give a little cause for concern.

"I'm sorry, Mum. I'll try harder," she promised.

"After all, it's you who's always saying that you must get high grades to get on to university," her mother reminded her, far from sternly. She moved towards the kitchen door. "However, there is apparently one subject in which your grades have sky-rocketed, although I can't imagine why . . ."

Lisa knew what was coming; she pretended to be watching the late-night documentary on TV. "Oh, and what's that?" she asked, trying (and failing) to sound casual.

"French," said Maddy, and vanished into the kitchen.

10

The following day was a Saturday and Lisa had decided to take the day off from studying to go into Applewood's main shopping mall for a spot of window-shopping. If she was lucky she might find the dress which she could wear to the summer ball; if she was even luckier she might be able to go back home and persuade her mother to buy it for her.

As she was walking down the main shopping street she looked casually into the window of Applewood's one and only record shop. Many of the students from college made a habit of meeting in there on Saturday afternoon; and more than once Lisa had been spotted by her friends and persuaded to go off with them to Brucianni's, the coffee shop in the centre of town which was frequented by all those who were seriously trendy, and many of those who aspired to be.

She glanced into the record shop and was disappointed to see that there was no one there she recognized. Oh well, it's no cappuccino and chocolate mousse pie down at the coffee shop for me today, she thought philosophically.

And then Lisa did a double-take. There was indeed someone there that she recognized; it was just that, taken out of the surroundings of the college, he looked so different, and, she had to admit, only a couple of years older than her rather than four. But nevertheless she would recognize those Chevignon jeans, that white Chipie T-shirt with the blue bandana tied casually around his neck, and that shock of thick black hair anywhere.

She walked into the shop and went over to the rock cassette section. She tapped him on the shoulder.

"Jean-Luc!" she said. "How are you?"

Jean-Luc turned round, and when he saw Lisa he beamed, and his brown eyes twinkled even more than Lisa would ever have thought possible.

"Lisa!" he said. "How nice to see you!" He meant it.

Lisa nodded to the cassette in Jean-Luc's hand. "What are you buying?" she asked.

Jean-Luc seemed slightly embarrassed, as though he was a little boy caught with his hand in his younger sister's bag of sweets. Nevertheless he showed Lisa the cover. It was the latest album from the Lower Depths, the art band whose praises she had extolled to him a few weeks ago.

"I thought you'd never heard of them?" Lisa asked a little suspiciously.

"Well, I haven't," he admitted. "But you seemed so much a fan of them that I thought I'd better find out why you liked them . . ." His voice trailed off.

Lisa couldn't help but smile. "Why, Jean-Luc, that's wonderful," she enthused.

An awkward silence fell between them, as suddenly neither of them knew what to say. Jean-Luc turned his eyes away from Lisa, and looked around the shop, as if he was scared that he might be spotted here.

As if being found in a record shop was a criminal offence for a teacher! he thought.

Lisa regarded the Frenchman with a dawning realization that Jean-Luc was scared of something. But what of? she asked herself. Surely not of me? What's wrong with bumping into just another pupil in a record shop on a Saturday afternoon?

Unless . . . unless I'm something more than a pupil to him . . .

Finally Jean-Luc returned to Lisa. "I'm surprised to see you here," he said casually. "I'd have imagined that you would have a Saturday job. We all of us have them in France."

"I should have," admitted Lisa. "I can't expect Mum to support me all through college . . . I suppose I'll have to get one in the school holidays . . ."

Another odd silence followed. It was easy for each of them to talk to each other at school; after all, what was more natural than for a student to talk to her teacher? But here, in that strange and

unpredictable environment which Chrissie liked
to describe as Real Life, things seemed to be a
little different, as if the pupil and the teacher
belonged to two different worlds, two worlds
which shouldn't really meet.

Think! What would Alison do in a situation like
this!

"Well, Lisa, it was nice seeing you," said Jean-
Luc.

"Yes. Well ..." said Lisa, and looked over towards the door. "I suppose I'd better be going
then ... I'll, uh, see you on Monday, Jean-
Luc ..."

She waved a reluctant goodbye and started
walking away.

"Lisa, wait!" Jean-Luc said.

Lisa spun around on her heels and looked
eagerly at Jean-Luc. Jean-Luc returned her gaze,
and nervously licked his lips, as he always did
when he was addressing a new and particularly
difficult class for the first time.

"Yes, Jean-Luc?"

"Don't go yet," he urged. "Look, let me buy this
cassette ... and then perhaps we can go for a
coffee. I believe there's a coffee shop near here
called Brucianni's?"

Lisa glanced down at her watch. "Well, I
suppose I've got the time ..." she said, knowing
perfectly well that for Jean-Luc she had all the
time in the world.

Brucianni's was a short five-minute walk away
and as they wandered down the crowded high

street Lisa was aware of people's heads turning as they passed them by.

Or, rather, of women's heads turning, for it was obvious to Lisa that most of the women shopping in Applewood this Saturday afternoon found Jean-Luc incredibly attractive. His dark Mediterranean good looks and stylish casualness singled him out from all of the other men on the street with their pasty faces and scruffy jeans and T-shirts.

The strangest thing, Lisa noticed, was that Jean-Luc appeared totally unaware of all the attention. All he seemed to want to do was to chat to Lisa about her tastes in music, films, books, food — the most inconsequential things Lisa could ever have imagined; for all he was concerned the female passers-by might not even have existed.

When they arrived at Brucianni's the place was packed and they had to wait several minutes before a table became free. As they stood in the queue Lisa looked around the coffee shop and recognized a few people from school, people she might briefly chat to on her way to lessons. They acknowledged her presence with a token wave and then returned to their conversations, now punctuated with giggles and knowing side-glances as they speculated on why Jean-Luc and Lisa were having coffee together.

Uh-oh, the rumours are really going to start flying around school on Monday morning, thought Lisa, with something approaching satisfaction. Nevertheless, she began to feel uncomfortable, but once again Jean-Luc seemed to think that there was nothing at all amiss.

"They probably think it's scandalous for a teacher and his pupil to be seen together," Lisa said, as Jean-Luc ordered coffee and cakes.

"Why?" asked Jean-Luc. "I like your company, Lisa, what's wrong with that? We like the same things, the same books, the same music—"

"You hadn't heard of the Lower Depths until I told you about them!" Lisa said and pointed to the cassette.

"Aha, but that is a mistake which I am now rectifying," Jean-Luc replied with a smile. "You're fun to be with, Lisa: intelligent and sensible too. Unlike the other girls at Applewood you're interested in more things than just make-up and who's number one in the pop charts."

"I'm interested in those things too," Lisa felt obliged to say, as Jean-Luc pulled a film magazine out of the chic backpack he had been carrying with him. Like many French people his age he was passionately interested in the cinema, and would snap up any publication concerning the movies. He opened it at the listings page.

"There's a special screening of *La Belle et La Bête* next Friday at the local art cinema," he said, referring to the famous French film version of the Beauty and the Beast legend.

"Jean Cocteau," Lisa said, remembering the name of the director of the movie. "I love him!" She had seen the classic black-and-white film before on late-night TV, and had been entranced by its fantastic special effects, and had even sobbed a little at its ending.

Jean-Luc smiled inwardly to himself. When everyone else her age was enthusing about the latest Arnold Schwarzenegger blood 'n' guts epic, or the most recent Hollywood psycho-killer horror, he might have known that Lisa Tyler would be the one to admire an old romantic black-and-white French fantasy film made as long ago as 1946.

"Do you want to go?" he asked hopefully.

Yes, was what Lisa thought.

What she said was: "Well, I don't know . . ."

Jean-Luc tutted and leant forward, across the table. For one brief second he rested his hand on hers.

"Please?" he said, and then added slyly: "It's all in French, so you can even pretend it's educational . . ."

Lisa giggled, and Jean-Luc took his hand away from her. Leave it there, please leave it there, she cried out silently.

"Friday night?"

"Friday night," he confirmed.

"Then it's a date!"

Jean-Luc leant back in his chair and smiled.

"Good!" he said, and added impishly: "You know, Lisa Tyler, recently you're easing up a lot more. You're beginning to realize that there are a lot more things in life than just studying for exams. Why, with a little bit of determination you might even start to enjoy yourself."

Lisa stuck her tongue out at the French assistant, and Jean-Luc cuffed her gently on the shoulder, almost — but not quite — as a brother would. They both burst out laughing and then Lisa felt someone tap her on the shoulder. She turned round, and her face fell.

"Having fun?" asked Alison who had just arrived in the coffee shop, laden down with shopping, most of which she'd charged to her father's credit card. She ignored Lisa and instead looked suspiciously at Jean-Luc.

"Good afternoon, Alison," Jean-Luc said wearily. The redhead had still not taken the hint and continued to pursue him; the flirt of the sixth form was now becoming a little tiresome. He glanced down at the film magazine. "Lisa and I were just discussing a movie we're going to see."

Jean-Luc, don't tell her of all people! thought Lisa urgently.

Alison's eyes narrowed and she flashed an evil glare at Lisa, before returning to Jean-Luc. For the first time since Jean-Luc's arrival at Applewood Alison had clearly got the hint.

"Oh, I see . . ." she said through gritted teeth, but nevertheless still managed to adopt a superior attitude. "French films? How very arty — I much prefer the latest Richard Gere . . ."

She smiled sweetly at Jean-Luc and said goodbye; before leaving the coffee shop she glared malevolently at Lisa.

"Jean-Luc, you shouldn't have told her that!" Lisa reproved as soon as Alison had left the place.

"Why ever not?" he said. "And if it means that she'll stop bothering me . . ."

"But she can be so spiteful when she wants to

be," Lisa protested, remembering what Chrissie had told her the other day.

"She'll get over her childish crush on me in a very little time," Jean-Luc assured her.

"She'll spread the news all around the school . . ."

"So what? What could be more natural than two friends going out to see a movie together?" He rested his hands reassuringly on Lisa's.

"You're my teacher, Jean-Luc! If the principal got to hear about it!"

Jean-Luc shook his head. "I'm the foreign language assistant," he corrected her. "And it's not as if we're about to start a raging affair, now, is it?"

"Well, no . . ." she said.

Jean-Luc's eyes twinkled as they looked into hers. "So relax, Lisa!" he said and then took on a stern tone: "And that is an order from your teacher!"

Lisa laughed and looked down at the table, as if to check with her own eyes what her other sense of touch was already screaming at her.

Jean-Luc had still not taken his hands away from hers.

11

The following Thursday Chrissie looked up at Lisa from the library table, which she had set up as a sort of counter for tickets to the summer ball.

"So you finally decided to go to the ball after all?" she said, as Lisa handed over her £12 for two tickets. "You finally decided to invite Train-Spotter James along, did you?"

Lisa gave her friend a wouldn't-you-like-to-know smile, and took the tickets. "I might have," she said sneakily. "And on the other hand I might not have . . ."

Chrissie hadn't seen Lisa so happy for a long time; there was a mischievous sparkle in her eyes.

"Don't say you've invited French Delight!" said Chrissie.

"Wait and see," Lisa teased, enjoying Chrissie's look of surprise. In fact, Lisa had invited no one yet; James would only be returning from university that coming weekend, and as for Jean-Luc, well, she would decide after tomorrow night when they had been to the cinema . . .

"You've gone and done it, haven't you! You've beaten Man-eater Alison at her own game!"

"No, I have not invited Jean-Luc," Lisa stated firmly and then grinned, pleased at the thought that she might have. "But what if I have? He's not a teacher, only the foreign language assistant—"

"That's not what you said the other week," Chrissie reminded her.

"Well, things have changed since then," she replied and was about to explain further, when Alison waltzed into the library.

Twice in the library in almost three weeks, thought Chrissie. For Alison Potter that must be some sort of record!

"Hello there," she said, positively oozing sweetness and light, which instantly made Chrissie suspicious, but went unnoticed by Lisa. She looked at the pile of tickets and mentioned the summer ball. Chrissie asked her who her partner was going to be.

Alison studied her nails and affected an air of nonchalance. "Oh, I haven't quite decided who the lucky boy is going to be yet," she claimed. She looked at Lisa. "And how are you looking forward to your date tomorrow night?"

Lisa blushed, while Chrissie was immediately interested.

"You have a date tomorrow night, Lisa?" she asked, surprised that Lisa hadn't confided in her.

"Not just any date," said Alison, scarcely able

to conceal the poison in her voice. "This one is with a certain cute-looking Frenchman."

"Lisa Tyler, talk about a dark horse!" Chrissie said admiringly.

"We're just going to see a movie, that's all!" protested Lisa, for once losing her temper. "What's so special about that?"

Alison shook her head. "The teacher and his pupil going out together after school hours," she tutted. "*And* without a chaperone, too! Why do you think Eliane was asked to leave? She was showing too much of an interest in the boys in the upper sixth, that's why."

Lisa and Chrissie looked at each other, uncertain whether Alison was telling the truth about Jean-Luc's predecessor or not. Alison fixed Lisa with a steely threatening gaze. "I don't know what would happen if the principal got to hear about Jean-Luc getting *involved* with one of his pupils . . ."

Lisa looked to Chrissie for support.

"Well, she's not going to hear about it, is she?" Chrissie said. "As long as you don't open your big mouth!"

"That's right — not unless I open my 'big mouth'," said Alison, and turned round and marched out of the library.

"Alison, wait!" said Lisa, and started to go after her. Chrissie stopped her.

"Forget about her, Lisa," she said.

"But what if she does tell the principal about me and Jean-Luc?" she asked. "He could lose his job . . ."

"You're just going to see a movie, and a French movie at that, like you said," Chrissie reminded her. "And what's so wrong with that? Listen, Lisa, Alison's only jealous. She'd jump at the chance for a night out with Jean-Luc . . ."

"But . . ."

Chrissie clamped a hand over Lisa's mouth. "No buts, Lisa Tyler!" she ordered. "You go to the movies tomorrow night – although why you want to see an old black-and-white French film baffles me. Don't let Alison stop you. You go out and have some fun for a change!"

Lisa followed Chrissie's advice. The following evening she and Jean-Luc had arranged to meet in Brucianni's and go on to the tiny art cinema from there.

Jean-Luc was sitting at a table, drinking a Coke and waiting for her as she arrived, perfectly on time. He was wearing a stylish black leather jacket, draped casually over his broad shoulders, a blue bandana, and a spotlessly white T-shirt with black 501s. It was the uniform which every other trendy male under thirty seemed to be wearing, but Jean-Luc carried the look off with typical Gallic panache and somehow stamped on it his very own style.

As Lisa came over to the table he stood up and kissed her twice on the cheeks in greeting. Lisa felt her heart leap in her breast.

"Lisa, you look wonderful," he said.

Lisa looked down at the soft pale green dress, which complemented nicely her long blonde hair, and the short and smart black jacket she was wearing.

"Oh this?" she said as casually as she could manage. "I've had it for years . . ."

As a matter of fact it took me three whole hours to get dressed tonight, she thought wryly.

"Well, you still look splendid," said Jean-Luc. "And I'm not the only one to think so."

"What do you mean?"

Jean-Luc indicated a boy sitting near the door, who was staring at her. As soon as she turned around he hastily returned to the book he was reading.

"He's been watching you ever since you came in," Jean-Luc explained. "He must be very jealous of me . . ."

Lisa smiled with even more embarrassment than the boy by the door was showing. She'd never been aware of turning anyone's head before; and now she found it was really rather pleasant.

Later, as they sat together in the small art cinema, Lisa realized how much she enjoyed the film of the horrible enchanted beast who falls in love with the selfless beauty. For the first few minutes of the movie, sitting there in the cramped and darkened space, she was terribly aware of Jean-Luc sitting close next to her, and his leg which would occasionally (and accidentally) brush against her own.

Jean-Luc, however, soon put her at ease as he

pointed out special effects in the film or nuances in the way the actors played their parts which she had missed the first time around. Lisa was impressed by his knowledge and his enthusiasm, and – when the film ended and she noticed his misty eyes – by his sensitivity.

"But I'm French!" he protested, as she teased him. "We're supposed to be romantic! And it was such a sad ending!"

"You're still a softie," maintained Lisa.

They walked through the throng of couples leaving the cinema to the car park where Jean-Luc's 2CV was parked. Jean-Luc suggested that he drive her home.

"There's no need to, Jean-Luc," she protested, rather unconvincingly.

Who am I kidding? she thought.

"I can catch the bus. And I live out of your way . . ."

"No, I insist!" said Jean-Luc. He looked at his Swatch. "It's half-past ten and it's a dark night . . .

"And this time Alison won't be in the passenger seat," he added, leading Lisa gently by the arm to the 2CV.

As they drove along – or rather, shuddered along, with Jean-Luc apologizing for the state of his battered old car – they chatted animatedly about everything imaginable, from music to films, and even gossiped about some of the teachers at school.

It seemed that Jean-Luc was regarded as something of an *enfant terrible* by several of the other teachers, who disapproved of the casual way he dressed and his winning ways with his students, all of whom he treated as his equals. He also confided in her that one of the female teachers had something of a crush on him.

"Mouldy Miss Rutherford?" Lisa giggled in amazement. The fifth-form maths teacher had always seemed such a fuddy-duddy. "Jean-Luc, she's over sixty and at least twice as big as a house . . ."

"Still, she invites me round all the time to her flat for 'tea and cakes'," he revealed. "Invitations which I have so far refused . . ." He turned off the main road and into Lisa's road. "I should not be telling you all this staff-room gossip, of course," he chuckled. "After all, I *am* your teacher . . ."

Lisa turned to look at him. "You're not a teacher, Jean-Luc," she said.

Jean-Luc parked the car opposite Lisa's house. It was now eleven o'clock, closing time for the pubs, and from off the main road they could hear the voices and laughter of Friday-night revellers on their way home.

The local pub, The Lamb and Flag, was popular with many students from Applewood, not least of all because the landlord there was prepared to turn a blind eye to people who were just a little under the legal age for drinking.

Lisa had often been there herself with Chrissie and Alison, although she usually stuck to orange juices or Cokes, while Alison would drink whatever was trendy at the moment.

Jean-Luc sat in the driver's seat, staring out into space. He tapped his long fingers on the steering wheel. There was an awkward silence before he nodded over to the front bay window of Lisa's house. The light was on.

"Your mother will be worrying about you, Lisa," he said.

Lisa was staring thoughtfully ahead. "What?" she asked, and turned to look at the curtained window. "Oh yeah . . . sure . . . I suppose I'd better go in then . . ."

"Yes, I suppose you'd better . . ." he repeated, without any conviction whatsoever in his voice. Neither of them wanted the other to leave.

Lisa unbuckled her seat-belt and looked at Jean-Luc; he was still staring straight ahead, trying not to look Lisa in the face.

"Thank you for a really lovely night, Jean-Luc," she began, and meant it. "I really enjoyed myself."

"So did I . . ."

Lisa leant over and kissed him goodbye on the cheek, as a good friend would. She frowned: was it her imagination or could she feel Jean-Luc tense up?

"See you in school then," she said, trying to sound nonchalant.

"Yes . . ."

She tried to open the passenger door, pulling on the door handle which refused to budge.

By her side, Jean-Luc clicked his tongue in

irritation. "It always does that," he said. "This car is getting old – I really should think of getting rid of it – let me try."

He leant over and tugged at the handle. With a grunt, he managed to release it and the passenger door clicked open.

"Thanks . . ."

"No problem . . ."

Jean-Luc looked up. His face was now very close to Lisa's and they looked deep into each other's eyes. Like magnet and iron their eyes locked together.

A second passed. Two.

They felt like an eternity.

Uncertainly Jean-Luc moved his lips closer to Lisa's. He paused for a brief half-instant, and looked even deeper into her blue eyes, as if to be sure that she was experiencing the same feelings he was.

Lisa's heart pounded with expectation. Its noise deafened her: she was convinced that the whole world must be able to hear it. But at the same time she knew that there was no other world, there were no other stars, no sun in the sky. Even the noise from the people leaving the pub could have been on a different planet, so oblivious was she to it.

Now there were no other people, there was only her, and Jean-Luc, alone, together. Nothing else mattered.

He kissed her, a long, tender kiss on the lips. His breath was warm and sweet and fresh, and his lips were soft and welcoming.

After what seemed unimaginable years later, but had only been a few seconds, Jean-Luc moved his lips away from Lisa's, while every part of her being screamed out for him to stay.

His black hair was mussed, and fell cutely over his forehead. There was a beatific smile on his face, as he gazed at her seductively with those dark but sparkling eyes.

No, not just seductively, thought Lisa. It's more than that. He's concerned. He wants to know that I'm happy. That I'm doing what I want to do. That I feel the same way as he does . . .

Is he crazy or what? Of course I do!

He brought his lips to hers again, this time with more passion. Jean-Luc cradled her face in his hands as Lisa wrapped her arms around him, pressing herself to him, feeling his body against hers, feeling his heart beat next to hers, breathing out as he breathed in.

She ran her fingers through his thick hair, and then along the outline of his firm jaw which was just starting to show the traces of late-night stubble.

He drew back from her again, and gazed into her eyes once more. Now Lisa found that she was smiling too. It was as if her whole life had been leading up to this one moment. This one moment with the gorgeous Frenchman, who cared for her, who liked her, who made her feel good and made her laugh, who . . .

He gave her a peck on the lips, and grinned.

"T'es belle, tu sais," he said. *You're beautiful, you know.*

"Et t'es beau aussi," she replied. *And so are you.*
He kissed her again on the lips.

"If you only knew how long I've been waiting to do this . . ." he admitted. "But I thought you weren't interested . . ."

Now it was Lisa's turn to kiss him on the lips.

"'Interested?'" she murmured. "From the very first moment when you played that dirty trick about the railway station on me, I knew that I loved — liked- you. You're so different from everyone else."

"And so are you," said Jean-Luc.

"But I thought that you'd go for someone like Alison or even Chrissie . . ."

Jean-Luc smiled. "And how—" he pecked her on the lips — "wrong—" and again — "you—" and again — "were!"

Gently, he kissed her again and nuzzled her neck. Lisa felt his hands run down the small of her back, sending thrills of delight through her entire body. At this moment she would have let Jean-Luc do anything to her.

Jean-Luc looked up, and smiled. "You must go home now, Lisa," he whispered softly. "Your mother will be waiting for you."

Lisa reluctantly released herself from his embrace. As she made for the door, Jean-Luc took her arm.

"I will see you tomorrow?" he asked urgently.

Lisa had a hundred and one things to do on Saturday: she had her homework and studying to do; she was supposed to go out for the afternoon with James, who had returned home from university earlier that day; she had the household chores to do.

"Of course," she breathed.

"I'll ring you tomorrow morning," he promised.

"But you don't have my phone number," she protested.

Jean-Luc grinned. "Oh yes I do," he confessed. "I took it from the records in the school office two weeks ago . . . I've been trying to pluck up the courage to use it ever since . . ."

Jean-Luc gave Lisa one final lingering kiss, and then let her go. She hurried up the short drive to her front door and then turned to watch Jean-Luc drive away in the battered old 2CV. As the car turned the corner Jean-Luc waved and blew her a kiss.

On the doorstep Lisa hugged herself, scarcely able to believe that what had just happened had not been a dream. Her lips still tasted of Jean-Luc's, and she could still smell his fresh aroma of soap and roses. She looked up at the stars in the clear night sky which somehow seemed bigger and brighter than ever before.

It's a dream come true, she thought; but I'm certainly not asleep!

Lisa took one final look at the street corner around which Jean-Luc's car had disappeared, and, with a sigh of decidedly French delight, turned and entered the house.

So caught up in her own emotions was Lisa that she failed to notice the person standing at the other end of the road. Alison Potter had been out at the Lamb and Flag and was now making her way home. When she noticed Jean-Luc's distinctive car parked outside Lisa's front door, she had made her excuses and left her group of friends.

Hidden in the shadows she had seen everything which had occurred between Lisa and Jean-Luc.

12

The following morning, Lisa's mother, Maddy, might have known there was something up. For a start, not only had Lisa got up at seven o'clock on one of the two mornings when she allowed herself a lie-in, but she had also spent over an hour in the bathroom.

When the doorbell rang at ten o'clock, Lisa was up and down to the door before Maddy even had time to put down the newspapers and get out of her chair.

"Don't worry, Mum," Lisa said breezily, as she rushed down the stairs leading to the front door. "It's only for me! I'll see you tonight!"

Earlier that morning, after Jean-Luc had rung, Lisa had said that she and Chrissie were going to go shopping down in London. They were aiming to catch the morning train, she had said, and make the fifty-minute journey down to the capital where they planned to spend the whole day and return late in the evening.

Maddy nodded knowingly; somehow the fine-cut designer jeans and brilliantly white blouse Lisa was wearing weren't the sort of things she could imagine her daughter wearing on a shopping expedition to the capital with her best friend.

Lisa opened the door to see Jean-Luc waiting for her. He was dressed once again in his black leather jacket, this time accompanied by a brilliantly blue shirt, open at the neck to reveal his chest hairs, and some stylish French black trousers. The early-morning sun was already bright and he was wearing a pair of Ray-Bans. He beamed when he saw her.

"You look wonderful," he said, and kissed her on the cheek. He handed her a small bouquet of roses. "For last night," he explained.

Lisa kissed him back, on the lips, to thank him.

"I could hardly believe last night happened," she admitted shyly, feeling like a third-former on her first date, and sniffed the flowers which smelt wonderful.

"Well, it did," he said happily. "And I for one am very glad it did." He offered her his arm. "And now may I escort madame to her car?" he said in a posh English accent.

Lisa affected a curtsy. "Why, monsieur, I'd be delighted," she said, and allowed herself to be led to the waiting green 2CV. Not quite a luxurious Rolls, she thought; but in the company of Jean-Luc it might as well be. "But where are we going?"

"To London of course," said Jean-Luc.

Well, at least that tallies with the story I've told Mum, Lisa thought gratefully.

"That sounds great, Jean-Luc," she agreed and then looked doubtfully at his car. "Do you think she's up to it?" she asked teasingly.

Jean-Luc took his arm away from Lisa's and gave her a playful punch in the side. "That car is the peak of French engineering precision!" he said.

Lisa winked at him. "That's what I'm worried about," she said, as Jean-Luc opened the passenger door for her.

As the car sped away the curtain in the bay window of Lisa's house was drawn aside. Maddy grinned to herself, not at all concerned that Lisa was hiding her new boyfriend from her.

Let Lisa keep her new boyfriend a secret for the time being, Maddy decided. After all, she had done the same thing almost twenty years ago when she had met a fellow student in her college bar, wanting to keep the relationship hidden and special for as long as possible, relishing the secrecy and privacy, and the joy of keeping him for herself.

Finally, of course, she had gone and married him.

The Royal Botanical Gardens at Kew, on the outskirts of London, make up one of the most beautiful places in the whole capital. Set in acres of greenery grow flowers from every corner of the world, and on a warm summer's day, with the sun shining down and glinting off the lily pools and ornamental ponds, it is the perfect place for a pair of new young lovers to stroll, ignoring the other tourists and just delighting in each other's presence.

As Lisa and Jean-Luc walked among the lanes of brightly-coloured flowers, their hands would brush against each other's. They joined hands automatically; it was some seconds before Lisa even realized that they were in fact walking hand in hand — it just seemed so much the natural thing to do that they had done it without even thinking. She and Jean-Luc were now no longer two separate people, they were a single entity, two halves who together made up a whole.

Jean-Luc led her to a pagoda, perched on top of a small hillock, from where they could look down on the people below. He had taken off his leather jacket and, as they sat down, he put his arm around Lisa.

She smiled dreamily, as his hand stroked her back, sending shudders of delight down her spine. The strong taut muscles of his biceps and the firm touch of his fingers massaging the small of her back made her feel as though she were in heaven.

She sighed: she still couldn't quite believe that this gorgeous, intelligent, kind man was actually sitting beside her — beside her, Lisa Tyler — and that he had actually kissed her and held her last night as if he would never let go.

"Are you happy, Lisa?" he asked softly.

"Are you kidding? I've never been happier in my life."

"Then I am pleased," he said in that peculiarly formalized English which he sometimes used unwittingly, and which only went to increase his considerable French charm. He looked her in the eye. "Because I think I may be falling in love with you—"

"Jean-Luc, I—"

Jean-Luc placed a finger on her lips to silence her.

"Let me finish," he said. "When I first came to Applewood you were the only one not to 'pursue' me. And I became intrigued. And as I became intrigued I learnt that, as well as being very beautiful, you were also very shy and lacked self-confidence. So I tried to build up your self-confidence, make you believe in yourself more. And as I did that so I found myself wanting to see more of you, spend more time with you. I wanted to know all about you, about your likes and dislikes—"

"Like the Lower Depths," Lisa interjected brightly, feeling slightly awkward. Very rarely did any of the boys at school express their emotions with such candour; after all, it wasn't quite the *British* thing to do. "And did you like them?"

Jean-Luc pouted sheepishly. "Well, actually, no . . ." He smirked. "In fact I hated them!"

"That's the trouble with the French," joked Lisa. "They might look good but when it comes to their taste in music – yuk!"

Jean-Luc pulled a face at her, and laughed. He pulled her closer to him, and Lisa snuggled at

116

his side, and with one hand teased at the chest hairs in the 'V' of his shirt.

She nodded down at the people below, all of them admiring the flowers and enjoying their day out; none of them knew her or Jean-Luc, and every single one of them was totally oblivious of their happiness. Jean-Luc realized what she was thinking.

"I would like them all to know how much I love you," he stated.

Lisa agreed, but still a worrying thought was nagging at her mind. She sat up and looked seriously at Jean-Luc.

"But Jean-Luc, we have to be careful," she urged. "Here in London it's OK, we can be what we want to be, do what we want to do . . ."

Struck by the concern in her voice, Jean-Luc took her hands in his. "What do you mean?"

"What would happen if they found out back at school?"

Jean-Luc shrugged. "Let them," he said with typically Gallic indifference. "I love you. What is the problem?" He smiled. "There is no problem."

Lisa sighed. Jean-Luc was like all Frenchmen, she decided; he followed his heart − he never thought of the situations it might lead him into. The French might be a passionate and happy race, she decided, but there was one thing which they lacked: basic common sense!

"You're a teacher—"

"I'm *not* your teacher, Lisa," Jean-Luc interrupted with what now had become a familiar cliché.

"But that's the way they'll see it," she explained. "You might lose your job—"

"There's only another three weeks of term left," he said. "So what is the problem?"

"So it might cause you problems back home in France," she said. "Or when you graduate and you want to become a teacher. What would they think of someone who's been going out with one of his students?"

Jean-Luc looked crestfallen. "Are you trying to say that you no longer want to see me?" he asked anxiously.

Lisa stroked his hands reassuringly. "Of course not. But let's just be a little careful for the few weeks we've got left of term. After all, we've got the whole of the summer holidays to look forward to, haven't we?"

Jean-Luc smiled and kissed Lisa on the forehead. "You know, Miss Tyler, at times you can be a very sensible and practical girl," he said affectionately.

"That's always been my trouble," she reflected, only half-jokingly. "But will you promise?"

Jean-Luc sulked playfully, trying – successfully – to look like a cute little boy, being told off by a particularly stern teacher.

"D'accord – OK," he said finally. "I promise."

"Good!"

"But when the summer holidays come, Lisa," he continued, "I would like you to come down to France with me . . . to meet my friends down in Cannes, see the place where I live."

"Jean-Luc, I can't afford that," she said. "Do you

know how much it costs to get a ticket down to the South of France?"

"We drive down," he said. "Just you and me together . . ."

Lisa looked warily at Jean-Luc. Here was this man — no, this absolutely gorgeous hunk — who she had kissed for the first time only last night, and who was now inviting her on holiday with him! Surely even for a Frenchman he was being a little too forward? Jean-Luc noticed her hesitation and laughed.

"You've no need to worry, Lisa!" he laughed. "If we go on holiday together I will not take advantage of you . . ."

" 'Take advantage of me'?" Lisa repeated. The words sounded as though they had come out of a particularly bad English novel from the 1950s (as a matter of fact, they had).

"That's right," he confirmed. "I will never — ever — make you do anything you do not wish to do . . . You are much too important for that."

He stood up and led her out of the pagoda, and back into the throng of holiday-makers and day-trippers. Some of them noticed Lisa and Jean-Luc as they walked hand-in-hand along the bright and fragrant flower-lanes of Kew Gardens. Those who did winked knowingly at each other: here were a young couple out for the day; a young couple who were very obviously very much in love.

"This is just too good to be true," Lisa murmured softly to Jean-Luc.

"What is?"

"You and me," she said and looked at him. "I mean, it seems unbelievable that someone like you shouldn't have a girlfriend . . ."

"I do now," he said simply.

And devastatingly, for Lisa.

"Are you sure that you haven't got some French stunner waiting for you back home in Cannes?" she asked, trying to keep her tone light and nonchalant, but praying for an answer in the negative.

Jean-Luc pressed her hand reassuringly.

"Of course I haven't," he said. "Otherwise why would I want you to come to Cannes with me for the summer?"

"Good point," Lisa conceded.

"And how about you, Miss Tyler?" he said mischievously, turning the tables on her. "Do you have some English hunk waiting for you somewhere?"

Now it was Lisa's turn to reassure Jean-Luc. "No, Jean-Luc," she said firmly, "I promise you that there is no one else . . ."

"Good." He stopped and turned to Lisa. "Because I don't think I could bear the thought of you being with anyone else, Lisa," he said, and took her in his arms. "If I knew that you were seeing someone else I couldn't even bear to be in the same country as the two of you."

He kissed her long and slowly on the lips, and Lisa responded with equal passion. All around them people walked past them and stared at them.

But for Lisa and Jean-Luc in their embrace, it didn't matter. For all they cared, they might as well have been on another planet.

13

Chrissie looked on disapprovingly as Lisa
bounced into the senior common room, her
face glowing and her eyes twinkling.

"Lisa Tyler, do you know what day it is?" she
quizzed her.

Lisa looked puzzled. "Why, Monday of course,"
she answered.

"Monday morning to be precise," Chrissie
corrected her. "And one of the greatest rules of
the entire universe is that no one – and I mean
absolutely no one – is allowed to look as happy as
you're looking on a Monday morning!"

Lisa blushed, giving away more than she
realized to Chrissie. "Do I really look so happy?"
she asked.

"Like the cat who got the cream – and didn't
put on an ounce either," Chrissie confirmed with
a grin.

"I must be full of the joys of summer," she said
flippantly, and pointed outside to the gloriously

blue and cloudless sky. It was going to be a long hot summer in Applewood – or so she thought.

Full of the joys of summer? Pull the other one, Chrissie thought knowingly, but said nothing.

There was every reason for Lisa to feel happy: she had just enjoyed the most wonderful weekend of her life. After they had spent the afternoon at Kew Gardens, Jean-Luc had driven her into central London, where he had treated her to a meal and then bought some cut-price tickets for one of the recent, more trendy musicals.

Lisa had protested at the expense and had even offered to share the costs, but Jean-Luc had insisted: nothing was too good for her, he declared, and even if he had to live on bread and water for the remaining weeks of term he was determined that Lisa was going to have a good time.

Lisa felt enormously pampered, treated like a princess, something she thought only happened in books or glossy American soap operas. It felt, she decided, pretty good; it was most definitely something she could get used to.

But the greatest thing about that Saturday was being away from Applewood. There in London, where no one knew them, and could disapprove, they were allowed to be themselves.

They could walk arm-in-arm through the crowds of shoppers in Harrods, safe in the knowledge that they weren't going to bump into Alison who, embittered by Jean-Luc's rejection of her, might decide to tell on them.

They could gaze lovingly at each other across

a dinner table, hands touching, and know that there was no possibility that Creepy Crowley might be eating at the adjacent table.

And when Jean-Luc suddenly stopped in the middle of Oxford Street, and pulled her close to him to kiss her, they were certain that Miss Bailey, the principal, wasn't going to leap out of the crowds and send Jean-Luc back home to France.

Returning home to Applewood, their farewell embrace in the car was so intense and passionate that Lisa thought she'd died and gone to heaven. When she entered the flat, Maddy had just smiled knowingly: she hadn't been fooled for an instant, but she was glad that her daughter had found someone she could be happy with. Lisa would tell her all about it in her own good time, she decided reasonably. And so what if her new boyfriend did seem a couple of years older than her? Maddy simply assumed that he was a student at the nearby technical institute, or the older brother of one of her classmates.

The following day, Jean-Luc had taken Lisa further afield — to the coast — where they had spent the day swimming in the warm sea or just sun-bathing on the sandy shore. It wasn't quite his home town of Cannes, he had told her, but it was the next best thing.

In a swimming costume Lisa had always been a little too self-conscious of her figure before, comparing it unfavourably to Alison's near-perfect physical proportions. With Jean-Luc, however, it somehow didn't seem to matter that she might have eaten one cream-cake too many the other day in Brucianni's.

Needless to say, Jean-Luc's body was firm and muscular, and he was an expert swimmer, the result, he said, of swimming in the sea every morning back home in the South of France.

"With all those beautiful, sun-bronzed, perfect bodies in Cannes, you have to stay in shape," he said, as they lay side by side on the beach.

"I thought you said appearances didn't matter!" protested Lisa and sat up. She viciously tweaked one of his chest hairs.

"Well, no . . ." he chuckled, "but they do help sometimes!"

And with that Lisa had stuck her tongue out at him and refused to talk to him until he had gone and bought her a strawberry ice cream and a Coke from the small kiosk on the promenade.

They had even made the acquaintance of some locals who came down to the beach every weekend, and had ended up playing a game of beach volleyball with them. For the first time in her life – and in the company of people who just assumed that she and Jean-Luc were together and thought nothing of it – Lisa felt that strange indescribable thrill of being treated as one half of a couple; and the words "Lisa and Jean-Luc" were suddenly imbued with a powerful sense of magic.

And how wonderful, also, did the words "my boyfriend" sound!

In fact, the only blot on an absolutely perfect weekend was that it had to end so early. Having successfully got out of seeing her next-door neighbour James on Saturday as she had promised, she had made an arrangement to see him on Sunday evening.

When Jean-Luc had asked her who she was meeting she had simply replied "an old school-friend who's at university", without mentioning their sex.

Of course there was nothing between her and James, she kept telling herself (at the same time trying hard to forget that kiss under the mistletoe last Christmas); but if Frenchmen were all they were said to be – and Jean-Luc seemed to be living proof of that – she didn't want to arouse his jealousy without good cause.

So their day ended early, with yet another passionate kiss in the car. And who cares who might be watching? Lisa thought recklessly. Jean-Luc had then driven off with a promise to see her tomorrow at college.

"And yes, Miss 'Sensible' Tyler," he had said, before moving off, "I will be discreet – in college at least!"

After a day out with Jean-Luc anything was bound to be an anti-climax. Tea at James's next door was doubly so. Still, Lisa did have a soft spot for James. Kind-hearted and awkwardly handsome in a college-boy sort of way, with short sandy hair, grey eyes and the sturdy body of a rugby player, he had always found Lisa attractive, and had clumsily pursued her for the past couple of years.

The trouble was, Lisa realized, he was just so boring, and didn't know how to treat a girl. Like many boys his age he had only recently discovered the attraction of the opposite sex; until then girls had been a minor inconvenience, getting in the way of his studies, his rugby games and his unfathomable passion for trains.

Even under the mistletoe, he had rarely asked Lisa about her interests or likes and dislikes; and his idea of taking a girl for a day out would probably be the local rugby match followed by hamburgers at McDonalds and a Sylvester Stallone film. In every way, in fact, he was the opposite of the caring, considerate Jean-Luc.

When Lisa finally left him, worn out and exhausted by his discussion of the finer points of the steam engine, she was looking forward to going to school the next day as she had never done before.

She also realized that for the first time in her school life she had let a weekend go by without doing one single piece of homework, or even opening a text book.

And for once, it didn't matter at all.

14

Monday was the day the fun-fair came to Blackchurch — a village about twenty minutes' bus-ride away from Applewood. It arrived every year, usually acting as a temptation for the college's students to forego revision for exams and tests, and go along and have a good time.

At the end of that afternoon's French lesson Jean-Luc had suggested that he and Lisa go and visit the fun-fair later that evening. Lisa was unsure: what if anybody from Applewood saw them there? she asked.

"Relax, Lisa," Jean-Luc reassured her. "Who is going to see us there? Some members of the third form perhaps? Are you seriously worried about their childish gossip?"

Lisa laughed. "No. But what if Chrissie saw us? Or anyone in your French class . . ."

It was Jean-Luc's turn to laugh now. "With the homework I've given them for tonight?" he said.

"They won't have time to watch TV let alone go over to Blackchurch!"

"Yes, that *was* a pretty vicious piece of homework you set us," she admitted. "Translate eight pages of a seventeenth-century play into idiomatic English, and all by tomorrow afternoon!"

"It will keep them busy for a while," he chuckled. "That was the whole idea!"

"But you've forgotten one thing," Lisa pointed out.

"Oh? And what is that?"

"I'm in the same class!" she said. "It's *my* homework as well!"

Jean-Luc winked at her. "But you, Mademoiselle Tyler, have the benefit of a private tutor!" he said, and hugged her close to him. Lisa pulled away.

"Jean-Luc!" she scolded. "Not here in the classroom!"

Jean-Luc's face fell. "Why ever not?" he asked. "I want to hold you. I want to show you what I feel towards you. And besides, there is no one else here. It is the end of Monday afternoon: all anyone is really interested in now is going home to catch *Neighbours*!"

"You crazy, crazy Frenchman," she said. "Start being sensible!"

"I'm French," he grinned. "I don't want to be sensible . . ."

"You're still my teacher, when all's said and done," Lisa reminded him.

"I'm not—"

"Yes, I know. 'I'm not your teacher, Lisa'," she

finished for him. "But that's how it's going to look. Heaven knows what I'm eventually going to tell my mum. Perhaps I could persuade her that you're the older brother of one of my friends. If you kept your mouth shut, and didn't let out that you're French, maybe she'd believe me . . ."

Who am I kidding? she thought. How could anyone possibly think that someone this good-looking, sexy, and chic could ever be English?

"Let us not worry about tomorrow," Jean-Luc urged her. "Let us think about tonight! Will you let me take you to the fun-fair?"

Lisa shrugged her shoulders in defeat. How could she — how could anyone — resist Jean-Luc, especially when he was looking at her with those big, pleading eyes of his, eyes which said that his entire future happiness would be destroyed if she didn't say yes?

"Well, OK . . ." she said, and Jean-Luc beamed and kissed her on the lips. As he drew away from her the door to the classroom clicked open. Lisa turned sharply around as she saw Mr Crowley standing there. He cleared his throat loudly and walked over to the teacher's desk.

Oh no, thought Lisa, what if he saw . . .

"I've left my books behind," he explained, as he rummaged through the drawers of the desk, seemingly oblivious to what had just been happening in the classroom. As he searched, Jean-Luc winked at Lisa.

See, he seemed to say, there's nothing to worry about at all!

"Eh bien, Mademoiselle Tyler," Jean-Luc said,

as Crowley started a conversation with him. *"A bientôt, oui?"*

"OK, Jean-Luc, I'll see you later," said Lisa, and reluctantly gathered up her schoolbooks.

While chattering to Jean-Luc, Crowley was still bent down, looking through the drawers for his misplaced books. Unseen by him Jean-Luc mouthed the words "half-past seven" to Lisa, who nodded and, with a smile of anticipation, left the room.

"Calm down, Lisa," Jean-Luc urged her later that night as he parked his battered 2CV in the car-park of the fairground. "You look as though you are in the middle of committing some great master-crime!"

"That's what I feel like," Lisa said only half-jokingly as she undid her seatbelt and thumped open her door on the passenger side. "Leading my teacher astray and getting him to take me to the fun-fair!"

"Aha," said Jean-Luc, and laughed, "I'm not your teacher – as I seem to keep telling you every minute of every day – and it was my idea to come here. So if anyone can be accused of leading anyone astray then it is me."

He got out of the car and looked searchingly at Lisa. "I do hope Mademoiselle Tyler approves?"

Lisa kissed him briefly on the lips. "Yes, Mademoiselle Tyler certainly *does* approve," she said, and felt a certain thrill kissing Jean-Luc in such a public place.

Unlike London, where they were certain not to bump into anyone they might know, here in

Blackchurch there was always the possibility that they might be seen by one of their friends. It gave the act of kissing each other a strangely pleasant sense of danger. Indeed, while half of Lisa was praying that they wouldn't be seen, the other half was secretly hoping that they would be discovered.

I want people to see us kissing, and loving each other, she thought. I want everyone in the whole wide world to know that I love you, and that you love me! I want to shout it from the rooftops! I want every single person at this fun-fair to see us together and to be jealous of us!

Jean-Luc looked around: already the park on which the fun-fair had camped was packed with young couples enjoying themselves. Trashy music blared from the loudspeaker systems of the various rides, mingling with the screams of pleasure of people on the big wheel and the dodgems. The air was filled with the familiar smells of freshly-cooked toffee apples, candy-floss, and burgers and hot dogs.

"So where do you want to go first?" he asked her.

What does it matter, she thought, as long as it's with you?

She shrugged. "I don't know," she said. "Perhaps the dodgem cars? Or maybe you'd like to win me a cuddly toy or a goldfish on the coconut shy?"

Jean-Luc seemed disappointed in her. "I have a much better idea!" he announced and took her by the hand, leading her through the crowds to the ghost train.

Lisa looked uncertain. "Come on, Jean-Luc!" she said. "Don't you think that I'm a little old for that now!" She looked at the youngsters getting on the ride: the oldest must have been about thirteen.

"One is never too old for the ghost train," Jean-Luc declared as he handed over his pound coins to the man in charge. "In fact the older you are the better!" He pulled Lisa into the last of the cars waiting on the track to enter the ghost train. As she sat down he put his arm around her.

"Now you don't really expect me to be scared by all this?" she asked, as the ghost train started up and they entered the ride.

Jean-Luc, his face very close to hers, shook his head, as they passed through the double doors into the darkened interior.

"Of course not," he said. "But one need not only be scared inside the ghost train . . ."

Just then, an enormous mechanical bat flew down from the ceiling at them, and Lisa screamed, in spite of herself. She clung to Jean-Luc, who held on to her tightly.

"I thought you said that you wouldn't be scared . . ." he chided.

Lisa laughed. "I'm not, but . . ." She looked into Jean-Luc's eyes; even in the dark she could see the lovelight gleam from them.

He moved his lips to hers, kissing her softly in the darkness. His arm slid up and down the small of her back sending tremors of delight throughout her whole body. He kissed her neck, burying his face in her long blonde hair.

Finally Jean-Luc released her from his embrace and looked affectionately down at her as the car rumbled on through the horrors of the ghost train.

"Are you still scared?" he asked.

Lisa pulled him back down onto her lips "Not with you around," she breathed.

"Then you shall never be scared for the rest of your life," he promised her. "I shall look after you – make sure that nothing ever harms you . . ."

And then he yelped as a skeleton rattled down from the ceiling, frightening the life out of him. His face was as white as a sheet. By his side Lisa burst into a fit of uncontrollable laughter.

"You're going to look after me, Jean-Luc?" she giggled. "Haven't you got that the wrong way round?"

"We will look after each other," he decided, and pulled Lisa close to him once more, and they melted gratefully and lovingly into each other's arms.

"Well, I'm waiting, Jean-Luc," Lisa said as she tapped her foot in mock irritation by the rifle range. "I want my cuddly toy!"

Beside her Jean-Luc was peering down the sights of a rifle at the rifle range, trying to hit the moving ducks before him. He had boldly declared that he was going to win a teddy-bear for Lisa at the rifle range and had discovered after he had paid his two pounds that as a marksman he was hopeless. He bit his lips, trying to concentrate, and fired, missing the moving ducks by feet. He sighed, and looked over to Lisa who was shaking her head in disappointment.

"I fall in love with the man—" she mused out loud.

In love! I finally said it!

"—and he can't even win me a cuddly toy."

Jean-Luc looked genuinely disappointed, which only made Lisa's heart go out to him even more.

"Alas," he said, "if I cannot win a teddy bear for the fair lady then perhaps she will not want me any more! How can she love someone who cannot even shoot straight!"

Caught up in the moment, Lisa pulled Jean-Luc over to her, and kissed him on the lips. She was suddenly serious.

"I love you for what you are, Jean-Luc," she said, surprising herself by her own boldness. "*And* for what you're not. You're not perfect – and neither am I. And that's what love is all about – recognizing a person's imperfections and *still* loving them."

"You're a very wise person, Lisa," Jean-Luc said and was about to embrace her once more when a familiar voice made Lisa freeze.

"Lisa! Jean-Luc! What a surprise!"

Oh no, thought Lisa, now we're done for!

Stuart Richardson, the blond-haired prize student from Lisa's French class, and his girlfriend, the willowy Helen, were standing in front of them.

"Er, hello, Stuart," said Jean-Luc while by his side Lisa flushed with embarrassment.

134

We've been found out now! Lisa said to herself. I knew it was too good to last . . .

"What are you two doing here?" he asked.

Long seconds passed. "I . . . I was here with Chrissie, and lost her," she lied, making a mental note to ring Chrissie the minute she got home so that she could confirm her story tomorrow. "And then I bumped into Jean-Luc . . . isn't that right, Jean-Luc?"

Jean-Luc nodded. "And as I was alone we decided to spend some time at the fair together . . . looking for Chrissie . . ."

Stuart frowned, as though he suspected that there was something not quite right with this explanation. "Oh, I see . . ." he said, plainly not seeing at all. He looked suspiciously at Lisa and Jean-Luc, and was about to say something when Helen pulled his arm.

"Come on, Stuart," she said. "I want to go on the ghost train!"

"You'll love that!" enthused Lisa. "We've just—" She corrected herself just in time – "Chrissie and I went on it before we got separated from each other . . ."

As Stuart let himself be led off by his girlfriend, Lisa breathed a sigh of relief while Jean-Luc just chuckled softly to himself. "That was close," she said. "I thought you said that the homework you set would keep everyone in tonight!"

"Aha, but Stuart is the top student in my class," Jean-Luc admitted, clearly not as perturbed by Stuart's meeting them as Lisa was. "If not the most important one . . ."

"At least it was him," Lisa said gratefully. "He's so besotted with Helen that he'll forget about the whole thing in ten minutes . . ."

Jean-Luc was looking around the fun-fair at the amazing selection of garish rides. He suddenly grabbed Lisa's hand and pulled her into the crowds.

"Jean-Luc, where are we going?" she asked.

"The perfect place to be alone," he said merrily, like an enthusiastic little boy going on his holidays. "I know the very place!"

Laughing and giggling Lisa followed as Jean-Luc pushed his way through the crowds to the Big Wheel. As Jean-Luc handed over his money to the operator Lisa looked up apprehensively at the Big Wheel. Jean-Luc took advantage of this to quickly slip the man a ten-pound note and whisper something into his ear.

"I don't know . . ." she said doubtfully. 'It's very high . . ." Lisa had always been a little scared of heights.

Jean-Luc put his arm around her waist and led her to one of the waiting buggies. "I shall protect you!" he said dramatically, like a cavalier in an old movie, as the operator made sure that they were securely fastened into the buggy. Jean-Luc winked conspiratorially at him. "With me by your side nothing can go wrong!"

With a grating and a clunk of gears the Big Wheel slowly began to creak into action, and the buggy containing Jean-Luc and Lisa started to rise into the air. Lisa trembled as the Wheel gathered speed, and let Jean-Luc pull her even more tightly to his warm and reassuring body. He kissed her.

"See?" he said, and glanced to the two empty buggies in front and behind them. "Up here we are alone: there is no-one to come and interrupt us! Scared now, Mademoiselle Tyler?" Jean-Luc asked.

"Not when I'm with you." She smiled, and then gasped as the buggy began to descend. "I think I've just left my stomach behind!" she laughed.

"No problem," said Jean-Luc. "We will just retrieve it on the next turn round."

The Big Wheel turned and Jean-Luc and Lisa's buggy began to rise again. By now Lisa was enjoying herself enormously: the thrill of the ride and the reassuring and loving presence of Jean-Luc beside her made for a wonderful experience.

They had just reached the top of the Wheel again when something seemed to go wrong. Their buggy lurched and shuddered, and the Big Wheel suddenly came to a jerky halt. A moan of noisy complaint came from the people riding in the other buggies.

"Jean-Luc!" Lisa said nervously, as they sat there in their buggy, suspended at the very top of the Big Wheel. "What's happened?"

"We've stopped," he said, rather unnecessarily. "Perhaps there's something wrong with the ride . . ."

Lisa noticed that Jean-Luc didn't seem overly concerned. "You mean we're stuck up here?"

Jean-Luc nodded, and kissed her on the cheek. "There's nothing to worry about," he reassured her. "I'm sure the operator will get it working again soon . . ."

Or in five minutes' time, to be precise, he thought. After all, that was the time we agreed on!

"Now sit back and relax, Lisa," he urged her. "Enjoy the view . . ."

"It's beautiful," said Lisa. From the top of the Wheel they had a magnificent view of the entire area. In the distance she could see the lights of Blackchurch town and farther off the lights of Applewood; and beyond them the black outline of the hills. Up here the stars seemed even closer and twinkled even more brightly.

She snuggled close to Jean-Luc, and smelt fresh roses and finely starched linen.

"I love you," she said. "When I'm with you nothing else matters . . . It doesn't matter that I'm not as attractive as someone like Alison . . ."

"Lisa," said Jean-Luc matter-of-factly. "Alison is merely attractive. You are beautiful." He stroked her blonde hair with his free hand.

Lisa smiled. "It doesn't matter that we have to keep our relationship a secret from the whole of Applewood . . ."

"Not up here we don't," he pointed out, and kissed her deeply on the lips. He glanced down at the revellers on the ground; they seemed like ants. "No one can see us up here."

"It doesn't even matter that we're stuck at the top of the Big Wheel!"

"Of course not," he agreed. "In fact at the moment there is no place I would rather be." He kissed her again and then turned her face gently to one side. He pointed to a streak of light in the sky. "Look, Lisa," he whispered. "A shooting star."

Lisa pooh-poohed Jean-Luc's suggestion. "Don't be silly!" she laughed. "It's not a shooting star; it's a firework. One of the men from the fun-fair must be letting them off."

Jean-Luc turned her face back to his and wagged an admonishing finger.

"Typically English! So unromantic!" he laughed. "You say it is a firework." He shook his head. "Well, I am French and I say that it is a shooting star. So a shooting star it shall be!"

Lisa chuckled; she could love this man to death! "OK, Jean-Luc, if you say so!"

"And in my country, whenever we see a shooting star we must make a wish," he said. He took Lisa in both his arms and held her fast. "And what do you wish for, Lisa?" he asked.

"Nothing . . ."

Jean-Luc frowned. "Nothing?" he asked. "One should not let an opportunity like a shooting star pass by so easily!"

Lisa looked into Jean-Luc's deep brown eyes. "There's nothing I want to wish for, Jean-Luc," she said and snuggled closer to him. "Because I have it all. I have you — and I realize that that's all I've ever really wanted. I love you, Jean-Luc."

"And I love you too, Lisa," he whispered, bringing his lips to hers. "And I will never ever let you go."

They kissed and kissed and kissed, holding each other tight, and staring deep into each other's eyes. They became oblivious to everything but each other, so that they didn't even notice when the Big Wheel creaked into motion again, and began its slow descent to the ground.

For Lisa and Jean-Luc there was only each other, alone together, floating high in the warm night sky, the only witness to their love the bright and boundless stars.

15

Alison Potter looked stunning this morning, Lisa and Chrissie decided, as the redhead waltzed confidently into the French classroom. (This was particularly galling as she had taken Monday off 'sick' – though Chrissie and Lisa suspected she'd been up rather too late on Sunday evening . . .) The class flirt normally wore outrageous, figure-hugging trendy clothes, which would make Cher seem overdressed and dowdy, and which blatantly displayed all the goods she had on offer to any interested boy (and with a good deal of success, it has to be said).

Today, however, she was wearing loose designer trousers, and an equally baggy but stylish white blouse. It was a drastic change of image, and ironically one which, while hiding everything that she normally flaunted, made her even more attractive. So successful was it that every man this morning – from the milkman on the doorstep to the school caretaker in the playground – hadn't been able to take his eyes off her.

She's up to something, thought Chrissie, as Alison waved at her and Lisa and sat down near them.

"Talk about a change of image," she whispered to Lisa. "From Supertart to Miss Demure overnight!"

Lisa, still on cloud nine from her visit to the fairground last night, just nodded and continued to stare thoughtfully at Alison.

She remembered something Jean-Luc had once said to her: "People who go about flaunting themselves are usually very superficial. I'm just not interested in them, no matter how attractive they might be."

An awful thought struck her: was Alison about to make another play for Jean-Luc?

Well, just let her try, Lisa thought, with a confidence she would never have felt until a few days ago. Jean-Luc has said he loves me. And she's definitely not his type. And there's nothing Alison Potter or anyone else in the whole world can do to change that.

The door to the classroom opened and Crowley walked in, followed by Jean-Luc. As they walked over to the teacher's desk, Jean-Luc turned to Lisa who was sitting in the front row, and gave her a tiny, almost imperceptible wink.

Lisa welled up with joy, delighting in their shared secret. But by her side Chrissie had also noticed Jean-Luc's gesture and instantly realized what had happened between the two of them.

And, unfortunately, so had Alison. And something inside the man-mad sixth-former seemed to snap.

142

An hour later when the lesson had ended and the class began to pack up their books and move on to their next lesson, Lisa went up to the teacher's desk where Jean-Luc was busy in conversation with Crowley. (They were speaking in English as Crowley had realized that, even though he was head of the modern languages department of Applewood, his French would never be as fluent as it should be.)

"Eh bien, bonjour, Mademoiselle Tyler," Jean-Luc said, and immediately regretted his mistake. He had called Lisa by her surname — when everyone in the entire school knew that he preferred to call every last one of his students by their first name! Why should he single Lisa out for such special treatment, unless he had something to hide?

He glanced over at Crowley. The French teacher was busy collecting up his books and class registers and didn't seem to have noticed anything. Jean-Luc kicked himself: he was just being paranoid!

"I've just been glancing at your homework," he said. "Your translation of Molière was very good . . ."

That's hardly surprising! thought Lisa. As you helped me out with it!

"Er . . . thank you for an interesting lesson, Jean-Luc," began Lisa, observing Crowley warily out of the corner of her eye.

"Je vous en prie, mademoiselle," said Jean-Luc awkwardly. "Don't mention it . . ." He also darted a covert look over at the elderly French teacher

who was taking an unbearably long time to leave the classroom.

Finally, after what seemed like hours of forced casual talk between Lisa and Jean-Luc — and what had actually only been thirty seconds — Crowley said: "Well, Monsieur Roupie, I'll see you this afternoon with the third form, shall I?"

"Oui, Monsieur Crowley," Jean-Luc said, and breathed a sigh of relief as the French teacher left the room. He turned round and grinned at Lisa.

"I've missed you," he whispered.

"You only said goodbye to me last night!" Lisa chuckled.

Jean-Luc fixed her with those hopeless puppy-dog eyes of his. "I know," he said. "I still missed you though."

Lisa looked briefly around to make sure that no one was eavesdropping on their conversation. Chrissie was looking curiously at them, but turned away when her eyes caught Lisa's.

"Well, I missed you too," she admitted. "I haven't been able to think of anything else but you . . ."

"By the way, did you meet your friend from university the other day?" asked Jean-Luc.

"My friend?" asked Lisa and then realized who Jean-Luc was talking about. "Oh yes, my friend . . . yes, I met them . . ." she said, careful not to reveal her friend's sex.

Jean-Luc looked searchingly at his girlfriend. "Lisa, is there anything wrong?"

"Wrong?" she asked, flustered. "Of course there's nothing wrong!"

Damn! Why hadn't she told him she was meeting James on Sunday evening? she asked herself furiously. There's nothing that I should feel guilty about! If he found out now he'd be certain that I was trying to hide something from him!

"When will I see you again?" she asked.

"Wednesday's French lesson?" he suggested, teasing her.

"You know what I mean!" Lisa smiled. "It's going to be so difficult getting a quiet moment with you at school."

"Ring me tonight," he suggested, "and we'll make a date." He took a piece of paper out of his folder, on which he scribbled down his telephone number, and passed it to Lisa. "I'll be waiting. And Lisa—"

"Yes?"

He looked deeply into her eyes. "I love—"

At that moment Alison, who had stayed behind in the classroom packing her books away into her smart leather backpack, came up to them.

"That will be all then, Mademoiselle Tyler," said Jean-Luc hurriedly.

"What's this?" asked Alison suspiciously, as Lisa quickly put the piece of paper in the back pocket of her jeans. "Love letters from the teacher?"

"Don't be silly, Alison!" Lisa laughed nervously, and added rather unconvincingly: "They're just the titles of some French books Jean-Luc's recommended to me . . ."

"Very conscientious I must say," said Alison snidely, giving Lisa a look which clearly said that she didn't believe a word of what she'd just been told.

Jean-Luc made a great show of looking at his Swatch. "I must go," he said to Lisa and added, purely for Alison's benefit: "I have a fourth-form class . . ."

"Goodbye, Jean-Luc," said Alison sweetly.

Lisa smiled weakly. "Goodbye, Jean-Luc . . ."

As soon as Jean-Luc had left the classroom Alison stared accusingly at Lisa. She folded her arms, the way the school principal did when a student was giving a particularly unconvincing excuse for being absent from school.

"OK then, Lisa, what are you playing at?"

" 'Playing at'? I don't know what you're talking about," said Lisa, knowing perfectly well just what Alison was talking about.

"You don't seriously expect me to believe that French Delight's just given you a list of books to read in French?"

"Of . . . of course he has," Lisa stammered. "What else would he give me?"

Alison didn't answer.

"So where were you on Saturday?" she demanded.

Lisa frowned. Surely there was no way that Alison could have found out that she and Jean-Luc had spent the day in London together?

"I went down to London with Chrissie," she said, repeating the story she had told her mother. "We went window-shopping . . ."

Alison tutted, shaking her head as though she was disappointed by Lisa's story.

"You'll have to do better than that, Lisa," she said. "You see, I rang you up on Saturday — I needed some help with my French homework — and that's what your mum told me . . . that you were down in London with Chrissie . . ."

Lisa shrugged. "So? That is what I was doing. What's the big problem?"

Alison smiled sadistically: she was obviously enjoying Lisa's discomfort. "The trouble is, Lisa, I met Chrissie for a coffee at Brucianni's on Saturday . . ."

"Ah . . ." Lisa suddenly wished that the ground would open up and swallow her. "Well . . . er . . . you see . . ." She searched her mind frantically for a half-way convincing explanation of her behaviour.

"Yes, Lisa?" Alison glared defiantly at Lisa, daring her to come up with a believable story.

"Look, Alison," she began in a comradely all-girls-together tone of voice, "swear you won't tell a soul, but you remember James . . ."

"How could I forget him?" said Alison, and added evilly: "I remember the two of you under the mistletoe at my Christmas party."

"Well, I met him over the weekend, and we went down to London together," she lied. "And because I didn't want anyone to know I told my mum that I was going down to London with Chrissie . . ."

Alison looked at Lisa through narrowed, disbelieving eyes.

"Oh, of course that must be it," she said sarcastically.

Lisa breathed a sigh of relief; for a moment she believed that Alison was going to buy her story. And then she added: "And I suppose you were with James on Friday night as well . . ."

"Friday night?" Lisa asked urgently.

Alison smiled and nodded her head.

"In the front seat of a certain green 2CV outside your front door. In the biggest clinch I've ever seen. Talk about tongue-tennis *à la française*! Come on, Lisa, get real! Don't pretend to me that you went down to London with boring old train-spotter James. It was Jean-Luc, wasn't it? You two are having an affair!"

"We are not having an affair!" Lisa protested. "We only spent the weekend together . . ." she protested, instantly regretting what she'd said, and how it might sound to someone like Alison.

"Aha! So I was right, wasn't I?"

"Look, Alison, keep it to yourself," Lisa pleaded. "If anyone finds out about us Jean-Luc is going to be in *big* trouble. He might even lose his job . . ."

"Yes, he might, mightn't he?" said Alison, regarding Lisa with a challenging look. "And what's more, if anyone were to hear that you were going out with the French teacher—"

"He's not a teacher," Lisa said automatically.

"If anyone were to hear that you were going out with the French *teacher*," Alison continued, "not only would he lose his job, and be sent back to France, but you might even be expelled."

Lisa felt her heart sinking and her legs shaking. She regarded Alison warily. Was the foxy redhead actually threatening her? She knew that Alison had been piqued when Jean-Luc had spurned her attentions, but would even she go this far?

"What are you trying to say, Alison?" she demanded nervously.

"Just one careless word, Lisa, that's all it would take . . . and it could happen so easily . . ."

"Are you threatening me?"

"As a matter of fact, yes," said Alison with all the affected sweetness of a King Cobra ready to strike. "Stay away from Jean-Luc, Lisa," she commanded. "He's not the one for someone like you."

"Someone like me!" Lisa snapped, uncharacteristically losing her temper. "Excuse me, Alison, but I don't see him taking you down to London for the day, or to the seaside! You tried your best to get your little claws into him and he showed absolutely no interest whatsoever! He doesn't just want someone who looks like she stepped out of a fashion magazine – he wants someone with a few brain cells to rub together as well!"

Alison stood there, unaffected by Lisa's sudden outburst.

"If I can't have him, Lisa, then no one else can," she declared evenly. "So if I so much as glimpse you two together again, if I even catch you staring dreamily into each other's eyes, then I'm going straight to the principal – to tell her all about our randy unprofessional French *teacher* who's gone and seduced one of his pupils! And if you tell Jean-Luc about it, well, I'll do it just the same!"

"You wouldn't dare!" said Lisa, although deep

down she knew that Alison was perfectly capable of carrying out her threat.

"Just try me," said Alison sweetly, as she slung her bag over her shoulder, and stalked out of the classroom.

"Lisa, is there anything wrong?" Jean-Luc asked, later that night. Even though he was at the other end of the phone Lisa could almost see the look of concern on his face. She glanced up guiltily at the clock in the hallway where the phone was: it was quarter to ten.

"Wrong, Jean-Luc?" she asked nervously. "Of course there's nothing wrong. Why should there be?"

"It's just that you promised this morning to ring me at home," he reminded her. "When you didn't I became worried."

"Jean-Luc, I'm sorry – I must have forgotten," she lied.

"Forgotten?" There was a sense of worried urgency in her boyfriend's voice.

"I've . . . uh . . . had so many things on my mind," Lisa flustered.

"Don't spend all your time on your schoolwork," Jean-Luc's unsuspecting voice laughed down the line. "I thought I'd cured you of that!"

"Yeah, well . . ." Lisa clenched her teeth; she hated doing this. But she believed Alison's threat: she had to protect herself, and Jean-Luc.

"Look it's not yet ten o'clock," Jean-Luc said. "Maybe I could drive round to your place and we could go and have a drink at The Lamb and Flag on the corner of your road!"

"You know I don't drink, Jean-Luc," Lisa said. What if Alison and her friends were drinking in the pub, as they were more than likely to be doing?

"Well, neither do I," he replied. "So we'll just have to share an orange juice and two straws there, won't we?"

There was nothing in the world that Lisa would have liked to have been doing more.

Instead she said: "Look, Jean-Luc, thanks for the offer . . . but I've got such a headache . . . I really think I ought to take an aspirin and get an early night . . ."

There was a disappointed silence at the end of the line. Finally Jean-Luc said: "Fine, Lisa, if that's how you feel . . ."

No, you gorgeous, gullible lovable Frenchman, that is not how I feel! Lisa longed to scream out.

"Yeah . . . an early night might do me good . . ."

"Very well. Perhaps tomorrow night then?" he suggested. "Maybe we could go and see a movie . . ."

"Maybe, Jean-Luc," Lisa replied. "I'll see you in school tomorrow . . ."

"*Bien sûr*," he said and paused for a moment. "And Lisa?"

"Yes, Jean-Luc?"

"I love you."

Lisa felt her whole being tremble. The very words she had longed to hear all her life!

"And I love you too," she said, and softly put down the receiver.

She lifted her eyes heavenwards and swore to herself.

Of course I love you, she said. And there's no one else I'd rather be going out with tonight, or tomorrow night, or for the rest of my life, for that matter. But for the next two weeks if Alison finds out that we're seeing each other it's going to be the end for both of us!

16

The French class the following morning was sheer torture for Lisa. Standing in front of the class, Jean-Luc was so near to her, and yet so unattainable.

She longed to rush out from behind her desk, and hold him in her arms; who cared what the rest of the class, the rest of the school, indeed the rest of the world thought? But sitting just a few places away from her was Alison, watching Lisa and Jean-Luc like an evil vulture ready to swoop down on her prey.

At the end of the period Jean-Luc called Lisa over to his desk. As Lisa approached him nervously she felt Alison's green witch-eyes boring into her back.

"Eh bien, Mademoiselle Tyler," Jean-Luc began, and consulted the class register pretending he was discussing Lisa's grades, "And how are you feeling this morning?"

Lisa cast a wary sideways glance at Alison

who was watching her. "Fine, Jean-Luc," she said.

"And how is your headache this morning?"

"My headache?" Lisa was puzzled.

"Yes, you said on the telephone that you had a headache," he whispered. "That's why you couldn't go out with me last night . . ."

"Oh of course, my headache!" Lisa remembered. "It's much better now!"

Jean-Luc frowned. He had the oddest suspicion that there was something Lisa wasn't telling him.

"Are you sure everything's all right?"

"Of course," she nodded furiously, as Alison walked past them and gave Jean-Luc a friendly wave. Jean-Luc waved back, and looked admiringly after the departing redhead.

"She dresses much better now," he said. "Less of those tight figure-hugging clothes. I wonder if she's finally realized that she's much more attractive when she's not being quite so forward all the time . . ."

Don't you believe that, Lisa shocked herself by thinking; even if she was wearing a nun's habit and acting like Mother Teresa there's no getting away from the fact that Alison Potter can be a scheming witch when she sets her mind to it! If she's dressing much more conservatively now you can bet that she's got an ulterior motive! And only you, you stupid crazy trusting Frenchman, who always likes to see the best in everyone, can't see that!

The classroom was now empty apart from her and Jean-Luc. He stood up and moved to Lisa's side of the desk.

"Maybe now that you're feeling better we can go out tonight," he suggested. "There's a new French movie showing at the art cinema." He raised his arms to embrace Lisa, but she froze at his touch.

"Lisa, what's the matter?" he asked, totally bewildered.

Lisa avoided his eyes. "Let's just play it cool for the next couple of weeks, Jean-Luc, OK?" she said, trying hard to keep her voice steady. Jean-Luc released her from his embrace.

God, I want you to hold me so much, she said to herself. I want you to hold me and just never let me go!

"It's all right," he said and tried to hold her again; she shrugged him off. "No one will see us . . ."

No one, only Alison Potter! she thought, and looked at her watch.

"Jean-Luc, I'm going to be late for my next class," she said in a trembling voice. "I'll see you later, OK?"

And with that she marched quickly through the open door so that Jean-Luc wouldn't see the tears, already welling up in her blue eyes. Behind her, Jean-Luc stood alone in the middle of the empty classroom, dumbfounded and deserted as the girl he loved ran off down the corridor.

Unseen by either of them in the corridor Alison smirked. Everything, so far, was going perfectly according to plan . . .

If that morning had been sheer torture for Lisa

155

then the rest of the week was a living hell. Whenever she and Jean-Luc were together, either in the classroom or even meeting casually in the corridor Alison seemed always to be there, too, watching them like a hawk.

Even when she wasn't there physically her presence poisoned Lisa's life at school. She longed to tell Jean-Luc of the threat the redhead had made towards her; but she was also afraid of the consequences. Alison Potter spurned was capable of anything.

Jean-Luc, for his part, was confused and depressed. Every time he asked Lisa if there was anything wrong, she would rapidly change the subject. Every time he tried to touch her, even on the arm, or kiss her in welcome, as all French people do, her body would become tense, and she would pull away, as though his very touch repulsed her.

Alison, on the other hand, had changed for the better, Jean-Luc noticed her more and more. Her style of dressing had become much more understated, and her former brazenness — which he detested in all women — now seemed but a dim memory. He had always known how physically attractive the sexy redhead was (no man at Applewood could fail to notice that!) but now that it seemed that she had given up any thoughts of pursuing him she seemed much more likeable too. Over the next few days he found himself having friendly chats or sharing a slightly risqué joke with her; she was, he decided, quite a nice girl after all.

But Lisa was still his main concern. Over the next few days she had used a variety of excuses for not seeing him after school. She had another headache, she had claimed, or too much home-work, or she had to accompany her mother to visit an elderly aunt. On Friday he thought he had finally succeeded: he had managed to get her to agree to meet him at Brucianni's coffee shop on Saturday evening. But at the very last moment she had phoned him to cancel: she had an essay to finish for Miss Greenwood, the Biology teacher, she'd said, and hurriedly hung up the phone, before he'd had a chance to question her.

So it happened that on Sunday evening there was an urgent knock on Lisa's front door. Maddy opened it, and silently gasped in appreciation, as she sized up the hunk on the doorstep.

If only I was twenty years younger she thought to herself.

"Good evening, Mrs Tyler," said Jean-Luc. "Is Lisa in?"

Maddy glanced behind her. Lisa was standing in the hallway.

"It's OK, Mum," she said. Maddy stood aside to let Jean-Luc pass, sizing him up appreciatively: the square determined jaw, the full lips and the shock of black hair; his strong wide shoulders and slim waist, forming the classic 'V' shape. She approved her daughter's good taste; that, at least, was one thing that Lisa had inherited from her mother!

She casually wondered why she'd never noticed him before; Lisa had hinted that she had met an older student from the nearby technical institute, and Maddy was surprised that she hadn't seen him on her way to work which passed by the institute.

Lisa led Jean-Luc into the living room, and closed the door so that Maddy wouldn't hear. She took a deep breath: she wasn't looking forward to what was coming.

"All right, Lisa," said Jean-Luc. "I think I deserve some explanations."

"Explanations?"

"Yes," he said, and there was a note of anger in his voice as well as a touch of sadness. "You've been avoiding me all week. I ask you to stay behind after class so we can talk, and you suddenly remember that you have a Chemistry assignment to complete. I ring you up to invite you out to the cinema, and you have another of your 'headaches'. And last night, when you finally agree to meet me at Brucianni's, you stand me up . . ."

"I had a Biology essay to finish for Miss Greenwood, I told you," Lisa said.

Jean-Luc shook his head. "No you didn't, Lisa," he stated quite categorically. "You see I rang Miss Greenwood this morning—"

"You've been checking up on me!" Lisa exclaimed.

"I rang her up about something totally different," he said. "But she told me that, as the school's summer ball is next week, she'd decided not to set any homework for any of her sixth-form classes . . ."

"Ah . . ." Lisa hung her head guiltily.

"You lied to me, Lisa," he said, and now there was real pain and anguish in his voice. "What is it? Don't you want to see me any more?"

"No, it's not that . . ." said Lisa, trying to avoid her boyfriend's eyes.

"Then what is it?" he demanded. "Are you in any sort of trouble? I love you, Lisa, and all I want to do is to help you if I can."

"I'm not in any sort of trouble, Jean-Luc," she reassured him.

"Then tell me what's wrong?"

Don't you think I want to tell you? Don't you think that I want to fall into your arms right now? Don't you think that I want the whole world to know that you love me and I love you!

"Jean-Luc, don't ask me," she pleaded. "Wait until term's over, and then we can sort things out . . ."

"I don't know if I can wait that long, Lisa," he said sadly. "You see, I believe in absolute honesty in a relationship . . ."

"Don't you think I do?" she snapped. I'm doing all this for you, she thought. Don't make it even harder on me!

"Then why can't you tell me why you've been avoiding me all week?" he asked. "I thought we had something special between us. That last weekend we spent together was one of the happiest of my life."

And mine, she thought.

"Another week, Jean-Luc," she said, "until term's over. That's all I'm asking you . . ."

Jean-Luc sighed and looked at Lisa through saddened and disappointed eyes. "Maybe you don't want to see me now?" he said, and added cruelly: "Maybe now that you've won the 'trophy' of going out with 'French Delight' you've lost interest in me?"

"No, Jean-Luc, no," she said, tears welling up in her eyes.

Jean-Luc moved towards the door. "No matter what you've done I still love you, Lisa," he said.

"And I love you too, Jean-Luc . . ."

He turned around and looked coldly at her. His big brown eyes were glistening.

"Well, you have a funny way of showing it, Lisa," he said and left the room.

Jean-Luc normally didn't touch alcohol, apart from the occasional glass of red wine at mealtimes, but tonight he decided he definitely needed a drink. He drove from Lisa's house to the nearby Lamb and Flag, and ordered himself a pint of lager.

Fifteen minutes later he shook his head, as he stared down at his almost empty pint glass. He couldn't understand Lisa at all, he decided. He loved her and she said she loved him; he had thought they were soulmates, bonded together not just by the same interests and passions, but by an indefinable *oneness*, each one half of the same coin. But how could he say that when Lisa wouldn't tell him what was troubling her or why she was avoiding him so much?

He walked over to the bar slightly unsteadily;

if he wasn't careful he was going to get drunk.

And what if I do? he thought angrily. I find the one girl I really love and think I might want to spend the rest of my life with and now she's trying to get rid of me!

There was a friendly tap on his shoulder, and he turned around to see the beaming face of Alison Potter.

"Hello, Jean-Luc," she said brightly. "Fancy meeting you here! What a coincidence — I was coming in here to meet some friends."

In fact it had been no coincidence at all. Alison had been walking home from a friend's house when she had noticed Jean-Luc's distinctive green 2CV parked in the pub's forecourt.

"Nice to see you, Alison," he said, genuinely meaning it. "Can I get you a drink?"

"The French teacher getting me a drink?" Alison said coyly, and grinned. "I'm only seventeen, you know. I'm not supposed to touch alcohol yet . . ." Which has never stopped me before, the redhead added to herself.

"Well, let's bend the rules a little this time," Jean-Luc suggested cheekily. "What would you like?"

"Oh, just a pineapple juice," Alison said. As Jean-Luc ordered the drink, the barman raised an enquiring eyebrow at Alison. This was the first time she had ever had anything non-alcoholic in this pub. Who could she possibly be out to impress this time?

Jean-Luc's seat had been taken by the time they returned from the bar and so they had to sit around a small table in a darkened corner of the pub. Soon they were chatting quite comfortably about general tittle-tattle and their likes and dislikes.

Jean-Luc was surprised to hear that Alison had been to the local art cinema the previous day to see a new French film, and she delighted in telling him all about it. The truth was that she had read a review of the movie in the local paper, and was merely repeating almost verbatim what the paper's reviewer had said.

No matter, she thought. It was obvious that Jean-Luc was impressed and believed he was discovering a previously undetected part of Alison's character.

Inevitably, by the time Jean-Luc had bought another lager and a pineapple juice, talk had got on to school. Alison asked Jean-Luc if he was going to the summer ball and disco next week.

"Alas!" he laughed, and gave her his sad puppy-dog smile, which he knew few women could resist. "No one has invited me!"

"You poor thing!" laughed Alison. *"Quelle dommage!"* She patted his knee in a sympathetic gesture. And left her hand there just a half-second longer than was proper.

"Maybe I should ask Miss Rutherford," he said, referring to the older teacher who had a crush on him.

Alison giggled at the thought of the fat maths teacher bopping the night away. "Can you imagine her dancing to the latest from the Lower Depths?" she asked.

"I can't imagine *myself* dancing to the latest

from the Lower Depths either," Jean-Luc smiled. "I hate them . . ."

"That's funny, so do I," said Alison, who was the Lower Depths' number-one fan. "And don't feel so bad about no one inviting you," she continued, "no one's invited me either . . ."

"I find that difficult to believe, Alison," said Jean-Luc, slurring his words just a little now as the alcohol started to take effect. "You're a very attractive girl . . ."

Alison laughed self-deprecatingly. "I feel left on the shelf," she laughed, and gave an exaggerated sigh. "Everyone's got a partner — apart from poor little me. Stuart Richardson's going with Helen Wilkinson, of course. Even Simon's going with Chrissie — although I think she only agreed to do it out of the kindness of her heart — I mean, who'd want to be seen dead with Si?" She eyed Jean-Luc warily, and took a deep breath.

"And of course Lisa will be going there with James—"

"*What?*" Jean-Luc asked urgently.

"Lisa Tyler," Alison replied. "She'll probably be taking James. He's back down from university for the summer holidays . . ."

"Who's James?"

"Oh, didn't you know?" asked Alison, all innocence. "They've been going out together since my Christmas party: you should have seen them under the mistletoe . . . They're practically engaged . . ."

Jean-Luc's face went white. "'And when did James come back from university?" he asked.

163

Alison pretended to consider the matter.

"Let me see," she began and stroked her chin thoughtfully. "It must have been last week . . . Why, Jean-Luc, what's the matter?"

Jean-Luc was staring into space: there was a tear in his eye which he angrily brushed away.

Everything had suddenly fallen into place – or so he thought: Lisa's off-handedness with him, her avoiding him and cancelling their date – it was all because James, her real boyfriend, had returned!

Lisa Tyler had made a total idiot of him! How she and James must have been laughing at him behind his back! He felt used and betrayed – and very, very angry. He took a long drink of his beer, and felt the alcohol go to his head.

"How would you feel, Alison," he said, "if someone you trusted completely, someone you thought cared for you – even loved you – suddenly went out and betrayed you? Made you a laughing stock?"

Alison looked into Jean-Luc's eyes, her face a picture of concern. She laid a sympathetic hand on his arm.

"I'd feel hurt and shattered, Jean-Luc," she said softly. "But I'd realize that life goes on. You've got to pick yourself up and get on with your life . . ." She began to massage his arm tenderly.

"So what if some girl has left you?" she continued. "If she was mad enough to do that then she's not worth your worrying about her."

"You're very kind, Alison," he said. Alison's face was now only a few inches away from his; she was smiling kindly at him, and her striking green eyes gazed longingly into his.

Softly their lips came together in an intense and passionate kiss. It was the sort of kiss that Alison was an expert at, and Jean-Luc felt himself being drawn into her embrace as a swimmer would be sucked into a whirlpool – or as a fly being dragged into the spider's web.

When Alison finally came up for air, she smiled. "I shouldn't be doing this," she said chastely. "Kissing my teacher in the pub . . ."

"I'm not your teacher, Alison," Jean-Luc told her, now noticeably slurring his words, and drew her closer to him.

Half an hour and several long and passionate embraces later, Alison made a great show of looking at her watch. It was late and it was time to go home, if she wanted to get up in time for school tomorrow.

"But what about the friends you were supposed to meet here?" asked Jean-Luc.

"Friends?" asked Alison, and then remembered the story she had told Jean-Luc. "Oh, it looks as though they changed their minds at the last minute." She looked lovingly at him. "And I'm glad they did. Otherwise I wouldn't have met you . . ."

Jean-Luc shakily rose to his feet. "Let me drive you home," he offered.

Alison shook her head. "You've drunk too much," she reminded him, and took him by the hand. "There's a taxi rank just down the road. I can get you a cab to take you home . . ."

They left the pub hand-in-hand, and as they waited for a taxi embraced once more – another long, deep and passionate kiss. Alison ran her fingers down Jean-Luc's back, sending tingles of delight down the Frenchman's spine.

"I feel so depressed and let-down, Alison," he confessed. "And I don't think I can face being alone tonight . . ."

"You'll feel better in the morning," Alison reassured him. "Much better . . ."

The following morning Jean-Luc drove into the school car park after having picked the 2CV up from the pub forecourt. As chance would have it he arrived just as Lisa and Chrissie were walking across the car park to the main school building. They both stopped and stared in amazement as Jean-Luc stepped out and sheepishly went around to the passenger side to allow Alison out.

Alison noticed Lisa and Chrissie and made a great show of kissing Jean-Luc passionately on the lips. Jean-Luc went off to the staff room, but Alison crossed over to Lisa and Chrissie. There was an unbelievably triumphant smile on her face: it was instantly obvious to the other two what Alison was smiling about.

"Hi there, girls," she said smugly.

"Alison, you haven't . . . you didn't . . ." Chrissie marvelled, briefly oblivious of Lisa's feelings.

Lisa was shaking, and darting a look of pure hatred at Alison.

Alison shrugged, and grinned enigmatically, a move which was calculated to say it all.

"I'll see you later," she said cheerfully. "I got up *sooooo* late this morning and I'm late for a class." She began to move away, and, as she passed by Lisa, whispered in her ear.

"I won," she said simply and cruelly. "And you lost."

17

"How could he do it, Chrissie?" Lisa asked through her tears as they sat on a bench on the lawn outside the Applewood school building. Fellow students, cheerful and bright in the early morning summer sunshine, stopped to look at her and whisper amongst themselves; but for once in her life Lisa couldn't care less what people thought of her. Her eyes were red and she let the tears run freely.

As soon as Alison had walked out of sight, Lisa had given voice to her emotions and broken down in tears. Chrissie had led her to the bench where Lisa poured out the whole story to her best friend in one long painful sob.

"We don't know what happened," said Chrissie. "They came into school together — so what?"

Lisa looked up. "Don't pretend, Chrissie," she said. "We both of us know what the truth is . . ."

Chrissie wasn't convinced, but said softly: "Don't blame Jean-Luc. It's that scheming cow

Alison's fault. She'll stop at nothing to get what she wants, and she doesn't care who gets hurt . . ."

"But what's going to happen to Jean-Luc now?" Lisa asked. Even in the midst of her own terrible anguish Lisa was still concerned with her boyfriend's welfare and reputation.

"With a little bit of luck, nothing," Chrissie decided. "If Alison wants to hold on to Jean-Luc then it's going to be in her own best interests to keep this thing as quiet as possible."

"But he can't love her," Lisa protested.

Chrissie hugged her friend. "Of course he doesn't," she reassured her. "But that's how men are — when they feel they've been betrayed they'll run to the first person who shows them any sign of affection. And when that person is a manipulative witch like Alison Potter . . ."

"I played right into her hands didn't I?" Lisa said bitterly.

Chrissie nodded. "But when Jean-Luc hears your side of the story, he'll change his mind — that is, if you still want him back."

"I want him back," Lisa said through her tears, With all my heart, she added to herself.

Lisa finally tracked down and cornered Jean-Luc in the corridor just as the twelve-thirty bell rang, and the corridor was filled with students hurrying out of their classrooms to lunch. Jean-Luc saw Lisa and instantly turned away, marching off briskly down the corridor.

"Jean-Luc, wait!" Lisa cried and ran after him.

169

She grabbed his arm, but he shrugged it off and turned around.

He looked at her through hurt and accusing eyes. "Yes?" he asked — a wealth of anger and recrimination in that one syllable.

"I have to talk to you, Jean-Luc," she said.

"So, go ahead and talk," he said frostily.

Lisa looked around at the hustle and bustle in the corridor as people rushed off to lunch; this was hardly the place to talk.

"Can't we go somewhere more private?" she pleaded.

"This is as good as any other place," he said soullessly.

"Look, Jean-Luc, I know how upset you must be," Lisa said — if you're as upset as me then your heart must be breaking, she thought. "But you have to understand why I've been avoiding you all this past week, why I've cancelled all our dates . . ."

Jean-Luc looked at her cynically, wondering what ingenious tale his former girlfriend was going to spin now.

"You're my teacher, Jean-Luc," she said and noticed sadly that, for the first time ever, Jean-Luc didn't contradict her as he usually did. "And Alison threatened to tell the principal that we were going out together. You could have lost your job . . . What I didn't realize was that she was after you as well and was determined to have you . . ."

There was a disappointed expression on Jean-Luc's face. "Is that it?" he laughed bitterly.

"What do you mean, 'is that it'?"

"You know, Lisa, you're going to have to do a whole lot better than that," he sneered.

"But it's the truth!" she protested.

"I thought I loved you, Lisa," he continued. "I thought I could trust you, and that you loved me too."

"But I do love you, Jean-Luc. You're the best thing that's ever happened to me!"

"And all along you were simply leading me on, using me as a little *divertissement*, a means of passing the time until something better came along."

Lisa was confused. "What do you mean?"

"You've made a fool of me, Lisa," he repeated, stubbornly refusing even to bring James's name to his lips, as if the very sound of it was repulsive to him. He looked at his Swatch. "And I have a lunch date . . ."

"With . . . with Alison?" asked Lisa, and found that her lips were trembling.

Jean-Luc looked at her defiantly. "Yes, as a matter of fact. With Alison."

He turned briskly away and walked off down the corridor, leaving Lisa alone amongst the crowds of students racing off for lunch.

That's it, she told herself with numbing finality. I've lost him for ever. Alison was right: she's won after all . . .

Her whole body was shaking, and yet she felt somehow detached from what she was experiencing, as if she was looking down on herself from a great height while her heart broke into tiny pieces.

171

She looked after the departing figure of Jean-Luc. We loved each other. I've kissed him, held him in my arms, told him my secrets. I know every curve of his body, know his smell, his touch, his everything ... And now he's grown cold on me, turned me out of his life for ever ...

She walked sadly off in the other direction. If she had looked behind her she would have seen Jean-Luc stop at the main door and turn around to look at her through misted and saddened eyes which even now were beginning to moisten with tears.

18

James looked at Lisa by his side, and decided she looked absolutely stunning. There was no doubt about it, he decided, something had happened to Lisa since he'd been away at university.

In that time she'd grown from being a studious, slightly bookish girl who hid her looks behind her glasses and her outdated hairstyle, to a beautiful and vibrant young woman. He'd always found Lisa attractive before; now he felt proud to be in her company, as envious male eyes stared in their direction.

He'd been surprised when she'd invited him to the summer ball, especially as Lisa very rarely went to such events. Still, he'd accepted with alacrity; maybe that kiss all those months ago at Christmas had had its desired effect at long last. Maybe Lisa had decided that she really did want to go out with him, after all.

Of course the reason behind Lisa's invitation was slightly different than the one he'd imagined.

After three long days of watching Lisa mope about the school, trying to avoid Jean-Luc wherever possible, and almost breaking into tears when she did see him, Chrissie had decided that her best friend needed taking in hand.

"You can't go on feeling sorry for yourself for ever," she had reprimanded Lisa on the way home from school one day. "You've got to try and forget him . . ."

"I loved him, Chrissie," Lisa said. "I still do."

"I know that," she replied sympathetically. "But life goes on with or without him. And we've got to get you back into the swing of normal sixth-form life as quickly as possible!"

Or you're going to drive me round the bend! she thought.

"And I know just the thing to take your mind off that Frenchman!" she added cheerfully.

"And what's that then?" Lisa asked doubtfully.

"You've still got your tickets for the ball and disco tomorrow," she said. "You paid me good money for them – it'd be a shame to let them go to waste."

"And who could I get to go with me at such short notice?" asked Lisa, who had originally bought the tickets in the hope that Jean-Luc would escort her. "Everyone chose their partners weeks ago."

"Well, I do know *one* person who would *love* to go with you . . ." said Chrissie, with a mischievous twinkle in her eyes.

"And who's that?"

Chrissie raised her hands in mock despair at

her best friend's lack of imagination. "Come on, Lisa, he's right under your nose – well, right next door anyway . . ."

"James!" asked Lisa in disbelief. "You're not seriously suggesting that I take James along?"

"Why not?" countered Chrissie. "He likes you a lot. And he's kind of cute – in a train-spotter sort of way. Besides he'll take your mind off Jean-Luc."

"I don't know . . ." Lisa sounded doubtful, but the idea did have some appeal. James had carried a torch for Lisa for ages, and would do anything for her. And Lisa remembered that kiss under the mistletoe: now *that* had been fun.

Chrissie looked engagingly at her friend. "Do it for me? It's not as if you're going to embark on a passionate romance with him, is it? You might even have some fun."

"Well, I'm not sure . . ."

"C'mon, Lisa Tyler," Chrissie said determinedly. "When have I ever given you bad advice!"

Plenty of times, thought Lisa, but eventually she agreed.

And so it was that Lisa and James made their entrance at the Applewood summer ball, dressed stylishly in the trendiest clothes their respective parents' credit cards could afford. Lisa was wearing a knee-length white cotton dress, bunched in at the waist with a wide leather belt, while James was wearing a sensible, but nevertheless trendy, black blazer, and Chinos.

The annual summer ball and disco was the one social event of the year when everyone made an all-out effort to dress to impress. Everyone was determined to outdo his or her friends, and each girl who entered the school's assembly hall — where the ball was being held — automatically scanned the room, to see who was wearing what. As the boys were also considered something of a crucial fashion accessory, they also looked to see who was with who.

The hall had been decked out in colourful bunting, and suspended from the ceiling was a huge net of balloons, which would be released at midnight when the disco officially ended. Couples sat at tables which lined the dance floor, and the air was alive with the sounds of the latest dance music.

A few of the younger, trendier teachers were in attendance — to keep a watchful but discreet eye over the proceedings. They seemed more concerned with interdepartmental gossip than with the students they were supposed to be supervising, and only left their own table when a particularly daring student from the upper sixth cajoled them onto the dance floor.

The teachers were also prepared to turn a blind eye to the alcohol which some of the students had discreetly brought in, even though about two-thirds of those present were still under eighteen. The teachers could hardly disapprove; many of them were only a few years older than the sixth-formers themselves and could still remember their own schooldays.

As the evening progressed Lisa found herself warming more and more to James and — as she was drinking orange juices and Cokes she couldn't even blame it on the alcohol — she started to remember why she had kissed him under the mistletoe.

A year at university had done him good, she realized. It had opened him out and made him realize that there was indeed life beyond Crewe railway station. He entertained her all night, delighting her with witty stories of campus life, or making her squirm with pleasurable disgust as he regaled her with descriptions of some of the things he had seen in his studies to become a doctor.

He was kind and considerate too, open about his affection for Lisa. What's more, he had learnt to dance. For James, this was quite an achievement, and it was one that Lisa fervently approved of. She loved to dance, and, as the evening wore on and she was caught up in the heady excitement of the ball, she found herself dancing closer and closer to James.

Looks like Chrissie was right after all, she told herself as they bopped to a track from another Australian soap star turned teeny idol. Coming here was a good idea — and I haven't thought about Jean-Luc once! She also remembered something Chrissie had said on the schoolbus a couple of months ago: James could be quite a catch. Maybe she was right about that too!

They finished dancing and joined Chrissie and Simon at their table. Chrissie and Simon had been getting on surprisingly well over the past few weeks, Lisa had remarked, and Chrissie had been regarding it as something of a challenge to rid Simon of his fascination with all things American. She hadn't *quite* succeeded – Si was wearing a Chicago Bears baseball shirt and jeans for the ball – but she was having fun trying. As they sat there chatting, Chrissie glanced towards the door at the couple who had just entered the hall.

Damn! she cursed. Why did they have to come – just when Lisa was starting to enjoy herself!

Alison was wearing the most expensive, most glamorous, most stylish – and reddest – dress of all the girls at the ball. And on her arm, dressed in a loose-fitting grey cotton suit and a plain black T-shirt, was the most handsome, hunky, and stylish man in the entire school.

One of the teachers in attendance raised an eye in surprise as he saw Alison and Jean-Luc cross the hall, and then shrugged.

I suppose it was inevitable, he decided, the sexiest sixth-former in the school, and the handsome young guy from the South of France. And what odds does it make? It's not as if he's her teacher . . .

Anyway, he had more important things to be getting on with, namely in the attractive shape of the young pretty English teacher opposite him.

Like all the other girls before her Alison surveyed the room, and then smiled, satisfied that she'd won yet again: the classiest dress – a little red Armani number which she'd bulldozed her father into buying for her – and the classiest guy! What more could a girl want? she asked herself.

Then she saw Chrissie's table, and her smile grew even wider. Alison couldn't believe her good fortune. Not only was Lisa here, in front of whom she could sadistically parade her new 'trophy', but so was James!

For the past few days Alison had been slightly worried that Jean-Luc might see through her little deception: it was obvious to her that he still had very strong feelings for his former girlfriend. So seeing Lisa and James together like this – and getting on very well, if you please – would finally give the truth to her lie.

She manoeuvred Jean-Luc over to their table.

"Well, hello there," she cooed. With all the sweetness and sincerity of a hyena ready to pounce, Chrissie thought.

The others mumbled their hellos. At Alison's side Jean-Luc tensed, and Alison wondered – for the first time – whether she had made a mistake.

Lisa looked away from her former boyfriend, until a not-too-subtle kick under the table from Chrissie forced her to acknowledge his presence.

"Uh ... hello, Jean-Luc," she said; what she thought was: Please, please leave Alison now. I love you and whatever misunderstanding there's been between us let's try and work it out together! I love you so much that I'd follow you to the ends of the earth if need be!

"Hello, Lisa," Jean-Luc's voice was cold and strained, as though he was trying to hide his true emotions. His jaw clenched and unclenched. He looked at Lisa and she was forced to avert her eyes from the anger and sadness in his.

"Have you met James, Jean-Luc?" Alison asked, trying to sound as casual as she could, but meaning: Have you met the man your girlfriend has been two-timing you for?

James nodded a perfunctory greeting and was perplexed when Jean-Luc glared at him. There was a dangerous glint in his eyes, which made both him and Lisa uneasy. He grunted an 'hello' to James.

"Sooooo nice meeting you," oozed Alison, casting a triumphant glance in Lisa's direction. "But we've come here to enjoy ourselves . . ." And with that catty comment she took Jean-Luc's arm and led him off to the dance floor.

"Cow!" said Chrissie.

"What do you mean?" asked James, taking his eyes off Alison as she wiggled off to the dance floor. "She's always seemed quite nice to me."

"Huh?" asked Simon simultaneously.

Only Chrissie noticed that Lisa was visibly shaken by the encounter. She looked disparagingly at the two men. "Look, why don't you two get us a couple of drinks?" she suggested.

"But you haven't finished," protested Simon, gesturing towards Chrissie and Lisa's unfinished Cokes.

There was a large potted palm behind Chrissie, an attempt by the ball's organizers to add a bit of sophistication to the event. She took her and Lisa's Cokes and poured them into the pot.

"We have now," she said.

James stood up and indicated that Si should do

the same. "I think we should go to the bar, Simon," he said, and looked questioningly at Lisa. "I think this is girl-talk . . ."

When the boys had gone Chrissie turned to Lisa.

"Are you OK?" she asked. Her friend's face was white and there were tears welling in her blue eyes.

"She's such a little witch!" Lisa said, and even Chrissie was taken aback by what for Lisa was very strong language indeed. "She blackmailed me into keeping our relationship a secret, and now here she is being blatant about her and Jean-Luc! And what's more" – she glanced at the group of teachers at their table near the doors – "it doesn't matter at all!"

"She's a cow," Chrissie said simply.

"You've got that right," agreed Lisa.

"So don't give her the satisfaction of knowing she's won," suggested Chrissie. "Enjoy yourself as much as you can tonight with James. When Alison sees that you're not concerned, who knows, maybe she'll even lose interest in Jean-Luc . . ."

"You really think so?" asked Lisa eagerly.

Chrissie shrugged.

For the rest of the evening the atmosphere was tense and electric. Unable to resist taunting Lisa further Alison would try and ensure that she and Jean-Luc were seen frequently with their arms around each other.

Chrissie, on the other hand, was fighting a losing battle to take Lisa's mind off them, steering her away to different parts of the dance floor whenever Alison and Jean-Luc came near. James just remained confused by the whole situation.

Alison's cloyingness was starting to irritate Jean-Luc and he would keep leaving the dance floor to get another drink from the bar. From the Cokes he had started drinking at the beginning of the evening he had graduated to the fruit punch into which some of the upper sixth had sneaked some alcohol.

As the evening drew on he and Alison would stand more and more by the bar, with Jean-Luc brooding, watching Lisa and James together on the dance floor.

Alison tugged at his arm, and gave him a worried peck on the cheek. "Lighten up, Jean-Luc," she encouraged.

Jean-Luc continued to look, not at Alison, but at the couple on the dance floor. He couldn't take his eyes off them.

"She said she loved me," he said, slurring his words slightly.

"But she cheated on you," Alison insisted on her lie. "Forget her, Jean-Luc . . ."

She took him by the hand, as the music changed tempo. The end of the evening was approaching, and the DJ had started playing slow smoochy songs. Alison led Jean-Luc out onto the dance floor and held him close to her as they swayed and moved to the now romantic music.

The dance floor was now full of embracing couples. Even Simon had persuaded Chrissie to join him on the floor, although she soon found herself regretting it as he stood on her toes for the tenth time. Sometime she was going to have to teach him how to dance. And funnily enough, she was rather looking forward to it . . .

Lisa and James were dancing too, and Lisa experienced a slight thrill as she felt James's hard firm body press against hers. James had made her feel good tonight, she realized, even though for most of the evening she had hardly been able to take her eyes off Jean-Luc and Alison as they danced close by. He was a good friend, and while he would never replace Jean-Luc in her affections, she found that she liked him a lot.

"I've enjoyed myself so much this evening, James," she whispered as she laid her head upon his shoulder. "Thank you."

"I should thank you," he said. "For inviting me. But there's been something bothering you all evening, Lisa. What is it?"

"It's nothing, James," she lied, painfully aware of how close Jean-Luc and Alison were.

"Because if there's anything I can do you only have to ask."

Lisa looked up and smiled at him. "You're very, very sweet, James . . ."

James bent down and kissed her on the lips.

And then suddenly several things happened at once.

Lisa felt herself being pulled rudely away from James's embrace. Jean-Luc pushed her to one side and launched himself into James, giving him a vicious blow to the jaw.

183

Jean-Luc was no match for the burly rugby-playing medical student, but the Frenchman's blow had taken James by surprise and he fell back into the crowd. He quickly reasserted himself and leapt up to defend himself against Jean-Luc, who was pounding away at his body. There was a wild look in Jean-Luc's eyes, and his face was reddened with alcohol. They both fell to the floor, rolling around on the dance floor, raining blows on each other.

"Jean-Luc stop!" screamed Lisa, as a crowd gathered around them. "Leave him alone!"

Obsessed with jealousy, and with his mind befuddled by the alcohol, Jean-Luc was deaf to her pleas. With a grunt James threw the Frenchman from off his body and staggered to his feet. There was a trickle of blood running down from the corner of his mouth.

"What do you think you're doing?" he barked, as Jean-Luc leapt to his feet.

"Stop it!" Lisa implored once more.

Two teachers had come over to the scene of the fracas and were holding Jean-Luc back from his rival. Jean-Luc shrugged them off angrily. He glared at Lisa, and ignored Alison, who had run after him in concern.

"I can't stand seeing the two of you together!" he cried.

"We were only *dancing* . . ." said Lisa defensively.

"I love you, Lisa!" announced Jean-Luc. "And I always will! Even when you two-time me with your boyfriend here!"

With a contemptuous snarl Jean-Luc stormed his way through the crowd and out of the hall. The spectators murmured almost approvingly amongst themselves: after all, this was the way all Frenchmen in love were supposed to behave.

Chrissie came up to Lisa and put a hand on her arm: she was trembling.

"Well, how does it feel to have two men fighting over you, Lisa?" she asked in an attempt to defuse the situation.

James joined them as well. "I'm sorry, Lisa," he said. "He just went for me. What's his problem?"

Lisa didn't answer, but Chrissie just shot James a scornful look: sometimes men could be such fools!

"I two-timed him with *James*?" Lisa said aloud to herself.

Chrissie looked accusingly at Alison, who was trying to hide herself in the crowd. Quite a few things were now beginning to fit together.

Lisa made a sudden decision. She ran out of the hall and into the car park, following Jean-Luc.

"Jean-Luc, wait!" she cried. "I have to talk to you!"

But his 2CV was already speeding out of the car park, leaving Lisa standing — alone and deserted — the summer rain falling down like tears.

19

Despite an early promise of long hot bright days the summer had turned into one of the worst ever at Applewood. Where the sun had once poured down like golden honey, now the rain threw down in torrents, and the wind blew mercilessly through the narrow streets of the town. The weather exactly matched Lisa's mood: dull, dark, dreary and despairing.

At eleven o'clock the morning following the summer ball Chrissie had gone round to Lisa's to see how her friend was feeling; and, more importantly, to give Lisa some good news.

After James had driven Lisa home after the ball, Chrissie had confronted Alison with her suspicion that she had lied to Jean-Luc to turn him against Lisa. Alison — ashen-faced and concerned that what, for her, had been a harmless bit of fun had ended in violence — had finally admitted her lie.

When Lisa heard the news she was overjoyed,

and immediately picked up the phone to ring Jean-Luc and explain the misunderstanding.

And that was the precise moment when Lisa's summer went horribly wrong.

"Can I speak to Jean-Luc, please?" she asked the woman on the other end of the line. She presumed she was her boyfriend's landlady, even though she had never met her.

There was a long pause at the other end of the line – an unsure hesitation. "Jean-Luc?" the woman asked grumpily. For her it was still early in the morning and Lisa's phone call had got her out of bed.

"Yes, that's right," said Lisa, growing increasingly impatient. "Jean-Luc Roupie. Tell him it's Lisa."

There was another pause. "I'm sorry, I can't do that, my dear," the landlady said, her tone softening as she recognized the concern in Lisa's voice.

"What do you mean?"

"Well . . . Mr Roupie left this morning . . ."

Lisa felt her heart sink. "Left?"

"That's right," said the landlady, more than eager to spread a bit of juicy gossip. "Came home last night – I think he'd been drinking. His suit was dirty as if he'd been rolling about on the floor, and his T-shirt was ripped . . . Anyway, he started to pack his things. He said he was going home . . ."

"Home?"

"Back to France . . . Still, he'd paid his rent in advance so I shouldn't complain . . ."

"Do you have his address in France?"

"Well, I don't know whether . . ."

"Do you have his address in France?" Lisa demanded, unprepared to put up with any opposition. "Please . . ."

"I'm sorry, but I haven't," said the landlady more softly, impressed by Lisa's obvious urgency at this point. If she had had Jean-Luc's French address she would have given it to Lisa. "He said that if he got any post I was to send it on to Applewood College, where he used to work . . . Do you know it?"

"Yes, I know it," said Lisa. And how! she thought.

"He said that the secretary there would forward it on to wherever he was staying . . . Is there anything wrong?"

"No, everything's perfectly OK," Lisa murmured, as she tried to stifle her tears, and hung up the phone.

Lisa turned to Chrissie and told her the news. Her friend's face fell when she learnt that Jean-Luc had left the country to return to France.

"Why?" Lisa asked desperately.

"If he thought that you were seeing James maybe he thought there was no point in staying in this country," she suggested. "And after his antics last night he wouldn't exactly be popular in the staff room, would he? And anyway, there's only one more week of term to go, so what's the point of staying?"

"I love him, Chrissie," Lisa declared boldly, trying hard to keep her voice steady. "And he

loves me. And now he's hundreds of miles away
. . . without ever knowing the truth . . ."

Chrissie moved forward to hug her best friend.
"Perhaps it's for the best?" she suggested, even
though she clearly didn't believe it; she added
reasonably: "After all, you live in England, he lives
in France, and you don't even know where . . ."

Lisa pulled away from Chrissie's hug. There
was a deadly serious expression on her face, an
expression so fierce and determined that it
actually made Chrissie shiver.

"It doesn't matter where he lives!" she
declared. "We belong together!"

Chrissie drew back. There was an urgency to
Lisa's words, a determination which she had
heard only a few times before, when the old Lisa –
the Lisa before Jean-Luc – had boldly announced
that she was going to get a B in her exams, and
surprised everyone (including herself) by ending
up with an A-plus.

Back then Chrissie had been impressed by her
friend's determination and her single-mindedness
of purpose. That same determination and single-
mindedness of purpose were apparent on Lisa's
face now.

"But there's nothing you can do, Lisa," she said
reasonably.

"Oh, isn't there?"

"No. It's the summer holidays in a week's
time," Chrissie continued. "Relax and enjoy yourself – it's the last time you'll be able to – next
year is exam year, and we're not going to have a
minute to ourselves."

"I can't let him go like this, Chrissie," Lisa claimed, "not knowing the truth . . ."

Chrissie looked kindly and sympathetically at her friend.

"Look, Lisa, he's a great and gorgeous guy, and what you had together was something special," she said. "And what Alison Potter did was evil — I doubt if anyone's even going to give her the time of day when what she did gets out — and I certainly mean to start telling everyone as soon as possible.

"But he's miles away from you now," she continued, sensibly. "And there'll be other boyfriends. Be glad for what you had with Jean-Luc, no matter how brief it was. Don't grieve for what you've lost: be happy for what you gained. And look to the future. James is really fond of you — he's a lot of fun — why not go out with him? You know he'd jump at the chance."

"No."

"C'mon, Lisa," Chrissie said softly, recognizing what her friend was going through. "Be practical — like you always used to be."

"No," Lisa repeated, and looked at Chrissie.

A sudden plan had already formed in Lisa's mind. She'd had enough of being practical, she decided, enough of being sensible. Now Lisa Tyler was going to do what she wanted to do, to do what her heart told her she had to do.

And so what if she ended up looking like a lovesick fool? Who cared what other people thought of her? If she didn't do what she wanted now she knew she would regret it for the rest of her life.

There was a look of steely resolve in her baby-blue eyes. Lisa remembered a conversation she had once had with her mother, Maddy.

"Chrissie, my mum told me once that she believed that in this life there is only one person for every one. Their *soulmate*, she called it. Without your soulmate you're incomplete. Well, Jean-Luc is *my* soulmate . . ."

"But Lisa, he's French," Chrissie protested, "he lives in another country . . ."

"So what?" said Lisa and shrugged. "We belong together. And if I can't have him then I don't want anyone else."

Chrissie shook her head despairingly. "Get real, Lisa," she said.

"No, Chrissie, for the first time in my life, I don't want to 'get real'," she said adamantly.

"For the first time in my life I know exactly what I want – and I intend to go out and get it."

"You've got a holiday job?" asked Maddy the following morning.

"That's right, Mum," said Lisa. "At Brucianni's. I'll be waiting on tables."

Maddy's face fell. "But Lisa, you don't have to. OK, I might not make the sort of money that Alison's parents do but I do bring home enough to provide you with pocket money for the summer. You've been working hard all through the summer term and you deserve a break – enjoy yourself."

Lisa shook her head. "No, Mum," she said self-righteously. "I think it's time I started supporting myself. You've done enough for me in the past."

"Lisa, is there anything wrong?" Maddy asked, full of concern.

"Wrong? Of course there isn't!"

Maddy looked enquiringly at her daughter. "No boyfriend trouble? That Jean-Luc person who came round the other week . . ."

Lisa coloured. "Oh, him . . ." she said nonchalantly.

'I haven't seen him around here before . . .'

"Oh, he's . . . he's a student at the institute, I told you before," Lisa lied. "He's gone home to France for the holidays."

"Oh, I see . . ." said Maddy uncertainly. She returned to the subject of Lisa's summer job.

"But you've never even had a Saturday job before," she pointed out.

"Then it's about time I started, isn't it?" Lisa said curtly. "And besides, I need to save money."

"Oh? And what for?"

Lisa thought fast. "Chrissie and I are thinking of taking a week or two off towards the end of the summer," she said. "Get away from Applewood for a few days, you know . . . James has these university friends who have a cottage in Dorset — he said we'd be welcome to stay there . . ."

Lisa looked warily at her mother.

"That'll be nice," Maddy said brightly, even though she was slightly put out that Lisa hadn't mentioned this to her before. "You need a holiday . . ."

My God, she's actually bought it! Lisa thought

with relief. Now all I have to do is to tell Chrissie!

The next two months passed incredibly slowly, as Lisa worked every hour possible at Brucianni's, waiting on the tables, and, when there was no work there, lending a hand behind the scenes in the kitchen.

She came home exhausted every evening, and Maddy wondered whether all the work she was putting in at the coffee shop was worth it. All the money Lisa was earning was all very well, she thought, but what was the point if she was too tired in the evenings to go out and spend it on enjoying herself? In the two months she had been working at the coffee shop she hadn't bought herself a new dress, or a new CD, or anything to show for all her hard work. Where was all the money going?

It was Chrissie who, towards the end of the two months, brought the matter up. She had hardly seen her best friend during the whole of the summer holidays; and there were times when she desperately needed to see Lisa, if only to escape from the attentions of Simon who had decided, after the summer ball, that Chrissie was the only girl for him. Strangely enough, as the weeks passed, Chrissie started to find his single-minded pursuit of her rather endearing.

She cornered Lisa as she was cleaning up a table at Brucianni's late on a Friday night.

"OK, Lisa, what's up?" Chrissie demanded. "I've hardly seen you at all during the summer holidays. In fact the only times I do see you are when I come in here for a cappuccino and chocolate fudge cake . . ."

Lisa smiled, and sat down at the table. "Chrissie, am I glad to see you! I've been meaning to ring you up for ages . . . only I never seem to have the time."

"I'm not surprised," Chrissie said disapprovingly. "According to your mum you're working two shifts a day here."

"I'm making lots of money," Lisa pointed out, "and I'm not spending any of it."

"It's not worth it, not at the expense of your social life," Chrissie said.

"Oh yes it is," said Lisa. "And besides, I'm finishing here tomorrow."

"Great. Then maybe we can go out together before the new term starts in a couple of weeks."

Lisa shook her head – she was suddenly very serious. "Listen, Chrissie, I need your help . . ."

Chrissie regarded her best friend suspiciously. She was up to something, of that there was no doubt. There was a determined expression on her face, that same determined look that had been on her face when Jean-Luc had left Applewood – almost two months ago.

"I've told my mum that you and I are going down to Dorset in a couple of days' time . . ."

This was news to Chrissie. "And I take it we're not?" she asked sarcastically.

"Chrissie, you've got to back me up on this one," Lisa pleaded. "Why do you think I've been working so hard over the holidays? . . . It's too important to me for me to be found out now . . ."

20

The train chugged slowly to a halt into the old railway station, and Lisa stumbled onto the platform, carrying her one piece of luggage — a large black leather holdall — containing two changes of clothes, some reading material, her Walkman and — most importantly of all — her passport and a French phrase book.

All around her people were milling and rushing about, leaving the train, or rudely pushing their way through the crowds to catch a commuter train which would take them from their jobs in the city to their homes in the suburbs.

Even concentrating as hard as she could, Lisa could barely understand their staccatto babble as they chatted and traded insults with each other in their own distinctive language and accents.

For the first time the enormity of what she had done struck Lisa like a bolt of lightning.

It was half-past five in the afternoon.

It was raining.

And she was alone in Paris!

The capital city in a country of almost fifty-five million people.

Fifty-five million!

And of those fifty-five million people she knew only one.

And he was in Cannes.

Another five hundred or so miles away.

Or at least she supposed he was. But Jean-Luc's home address, which she had sneakily obtained from the school secretary by saying that she had promised to send the French assistant some English books, was the only clue to the whereabouts of the man she loved above all else, and for whom she'd spent the entire savings from her holiday job to finance this trip to France and track him down.

It hadn't been easy, or comfortable, fooling her mother into thinking that she was going to Dorset for a fortnight's holiday. She had needed Chrissie to back her up every step of the way. And fortunately Chrissie — when she wasn't gleefully spreading juicy gossip around the school — was a loving and loyal friend, and had backed her story.

By a stroke of luck, Chrissie herself was going to be away from Applewood for the two weeks Lisa was away anyway, which substantiated Lisa's story even further.

"But don't tell anyone who I'm going away with!" Chrissie had begged Lisa. After all, it wouldn't have done Chrissie's image any good at all for it to be known that she was going on holiday with the so retro-cool-it-was-painful Simon who, after stepping on her feet for the umpteenth time at the school summer ball, had since then somehow captured her heart with his charmingly total lack of charm . . .

The train journey down to Dover and the ferry trip across to Calais had been easy enough. Even the connection to Paris had been trouble-free as she had been befriended by a group of English tourists who had done the Channel crossing many times before. But now the tourists had gone on their way and Lisa was alone, in a country of foreigners, none of whom, she decided, spoke – or wanted to speak – English.

She stumbled through the crowds at the Gare du Nord railway station to look for a map of the city. She remembered what Jean-Luc had told her, all those months ago when he had called her up in front of the class and played his little joke on her. Like London, Paris has several different railway stations, he had said, each one of which services a different part of the country.

C'mon, Lisa, think! she urged herself. Which is the one which takes you down to the South of France? Why didn't you pay attention in class?

Because I was too busy staring into Jean-Luc's deep brown eyes, that's why, she answered herself.

She looked cluelessly up at a map on the wall, hoping that a name would ring a bell in her mind. The Gare Saint-Lazare, the Gare de Lyon, the Gare de l'Est, the Gare d'Austerlitz . . . None of them sounded familiar.

She turned in desperation to a good-looking, trendy young man who was also studying the map. Back home in England he would have been declared a drop-dead, to-die-for hunk; here in Paris, he was just another good-looking, stylish Frenchman.

"*Eh, pardon, monsieur,*" she began in her hesitant schoolgirl French, "*je veux . . . prendre le train pour Cannes. Vous . . . savez . . . ?*"

Her French dried up. Why was it that in the classroom, talking to Jean-Luc, she could always get top marks; but here in Paris, talking to a real live Parisian, she fell flat on her face?

The Frenchman smiled generously at her, amused by her attempts at speaking his native tongue. "Perhaps you'd better try in your own language?" he suggested in a heavily-accented English.

Lisa breathed a sigh of relief. "I'm trying to get to Cannes," she said. "Which train station must I go to?"

"Why, the Gare de Lyon, of course," he answered, eyeing Lisa up appreciatively.

"And how can I get there?" she asked urgently.

"It's quite simple, mademoiselle," he said, "you must take the Metro. Travel on line number five to the Bastille, and then change to line number one for the Gare de Lyon . . ."

Number five to the Bastille, number one to the railway station, Lisa recited to herself, over and over like a mantra.

"But I have a far better idea," the man began.

"And what's that?" Lisa asked innocently,

thinking that the Frenchman might be prepared to offer her a lift.

"You are alone in Paris," he said flirtatiously. "Forget about Cannes. There is a nice little bar I know around the corner. Come and have a drink with me. There we can get to know each other better . . . You are a very attractive woman . . ."

Lisa's face fell. Only a few hours in this country and already the men were coming on to her! Maybe what everyone always said about Frenchmen was true after all!

The Frenchman shrugged. "Ah well, if mademoiselle chooses not to enjoy my company, what can I do?" he said helplessly. "At the very least I can help you carry your luggage to the Metro . . ."

"No thank you," Lisa said primly. "I can manage that perfectly well myself, thank you very much . . ."

"Do not be so English," the Frenchman said. "You are in France now. We do not have so many — how do you say? — 'hang-ups' as you British." And ignoring Lisa's protests he picked up her bag and led her down to the Metro station.

If Chrissie were here now, thought Lisa, she'd say I'm mad — turning down a date with a handsome young Parisian! And how different he is from the English boys. Turn them down, and they're off looking for the next female to chat up. This one offers to carry my suitcase! There was something very different about the French which Lisa liked very much indeed.

After the young man had seen her safely on the Metro to the Bastille she looked around at her fellow passengers in the railway carriage. They were all, men and women, dressed in chic fashions, and every last one of them carried about them that air of casual elegance and sophistication which only the French have.

Many of them were dark and Latin-looking and Lisa, with her fresh-faced complexion, blonde hair and clothes bought from one of the chain stores at Applewood, felt very out of place indeed. Curious French eyes started to stare at this stranger in their midst and Lisa was beginning to feel very awkward when the Metro train lurched to a halt at the Bastille Metro station and crowds poured out of the train, almost knocking Lisa to the ground.

Safely on the platform, Lisa looked around for any indication of where to go next to change trains. The times she had been to London – without Jean-Luc – she had hated the Underground system there, finding its complicated network of interconnecting railway lines confusing for anyone who didn't live there and travel on the system every day of his life. The Paris Metro system had the added disadvantage, thought Lisa, of being entirely French: like Jean-Luc's 2CV it was undeniably fast and efficient – if you could only work out how to use it!

Finally she found the platform for trains on Metro line one and thankfully slumped into a seat with her luggage, as the train started thundering through the tunnels in the direction of what she thought was the Gare de Lyon. It was only when Lisa had been on the train for fifteen minutes or so and had just passed the Champs Elysées Metro station that she decided that something was wrong.

She turned to the person sitting next to her, a chic and glamorous fifty something woman reading a copy of French *Vogue*, and asked her when they would be reaching the Gare de Lyon.

The fifty something woman smiled sympathetically at Lisa with all the slightly patronizing affection that big-city dwellers reserve for naïve out-of-towners.

"But you're going in completely the wrong direction, my dear," she said in French. "This train is going west. You need to go east . . ."

Lisa felt her heart sink. Here she was, trying to cross an entire country and she couldn't even find her way across town! Maybe her whole trip was doomed from the outset. Tired and exhausted after her long train and ferry trip, she felt herself close to tears.

The woman looked curiously at her. "What is wrong, my child?" she asked curiously.

Grateful for a friendly ear Lisa poured out the whole story of her and Jean-Luc, once again discovering that, when speaking a foreign language, she wasn't half as embarrassed about openly discussing her innermost feelings.

As Lisa told her tale the woman started to smile, and by the time she had finished there was a sympathetic tear in the woman's eye.

"Aha, such courage, such daring! Such love!" she said admiringly. "And who said the British were cold and boring? No wonder he loves you!"

"You really think I'm doing the right thing?" asked Lisa, who had been trying to ignore her doubts all the way down to Paris.

"Of course!" said the woman with conviction. "*Il faut toujours suivre le coeur!* You must always – always – do what your heart tells you, no matter what common sense or others advise!"

As the train rumbled to a halt at the next Metro station the woman stood up and took Lisa's hand. Lisa looked enquiringly at her.

"You have inspired me!" the fifty something woman declared. "Follow me!"

"But where are we going?" asked Lisa, impressed and slightly bemused by the woman's over-the-top attitude. Undoubtedly Lisa reminded her of her own long-lost youth.

"We are getting a taxi," she said. "I am taking you to the Gare de Lyon myself! Nothing – absolutely nothing – must be allowed to stand in the way of true love!"

21

Even with the dry and refreshing Mistral – the wind that blows on from the mountains down to the Mediterranean coast – the heat was oppressive when Lisa disembarked at Cannes railway station early the following morning after the long overnight haul from the Gare de Lyon in Paris to the trendy French town on the Côte d'Azur.

In the distance Lisa could hear the bustling sounds of market porters as they carried their wares to the city market, and the squawks and cries of seagulls as they wheeled and swooped in the blue and cloudless sky.

There was a scent of lavender in the air, and from the café across the road she could smell the wonderful early-morning aroma of freshly-baked bread. Compared to Applewood, or Paris – or rather the little she had seen of it from the window of a Metro carriage or a taxi – with its fuggy smell of car exhausts and American hot dogs, this place was like a heaven on earth.

And somewhere, maybe even just around the corner, there's an angel! she thought.

Clutched tightly in her hand was the scrap of paper on which she had written Jean-Luc's address in Cannes, which she had cajoled the school secretary into giving her: Flat One, 37 rue de la Châtelaine. Although Jean-Luc had told her that his mother lived on the outskirts of the town, he had a flat very near the centre of town. Lisa presumed he shared the flat with other students: she only prayed that he hadn't given up his room in the flat when he had moved to England.

She looked at the notice on the door of the tourist bureau at the railway station. The office wouldn't be open until half-past seven, which meant that she had another hour to wait until she could buy a map of the town and find out the exact location of Jean-Luc's road.

She mentally kicked herself for not having bought a map of Cannes in Paris, or even in England. That was something that the old, sensible and practical Lisa would have done, she told herself; on the other hand, the old, sensible and practical Lisa wouldn't have suddenly taken it into her head to travel all the way down to the South of France in pursuit of the man she loved.

She crossed over the road – narrowly avoiding the cars which were being driven by drivers who had a typically French disregard for the safety of the pedestrian – and entered the café shop opposite. Even this early in the morning it was full of workers from the nearby market, or young backpackers on their way to the coast, who had disembarked from the railway station. There was no free table so she asked if she could share the table of a boy and a girl who were about her own age.

"*Bien sûr*," agreed the girl – a slight, elfin-faced creature with sandy-coloured hair – and offered Lisa a seat.

As the waitress came to take Lisa's order of a chocolate croissant and a café au lait, the girl introduced herself as Lydie, and the young handsome dark-haired boy by her side as her brother, Christophe. They were both science students at the famous Sorbonne University in Paris, Lydie told them; but every summer, in common with so many other Parisians, they came down to the Côte d'Azur where their parents owned a holiday apartment.

"And you, you are from England?" asked Christophe in his faltering English.

"That's right."

"And have you come down for a holiday too?" asked Lydie, whose English was considerably better than her brother's.

"Well ... not exactly ..." said Lisa slightly embarrassed.

"You should do," urged Christophe. "The Mediterranean is beautiful this time of the year. The sun always shines, you can go wind-surfing or water skiing ..."

"And the beaches are always crowded," said Lydie, and added, "with such good-looking men!" The two girls giggled conspiratorially.

"I'm not interested in chasing any good-looking men along the Croisette," said Lisa, remembering the name Jean-Luc had given to the main boulevard along the seafront at Cannes. She bit into her croissant: it was delicious.

Lydie looked interested. "Oh?" she asked. "And then for what have you come to Cannes?"

Lisa looked slightly embarrassed, and lowered her eyes. Considered dispassionately, her quest to find Jean-Luc might sound laughable to strangers. But when she looked up, after having told Lydie and Christophe the story of her and Jean-Luc and of Alison's evil trick she found that both of them were beaming.

"That is wonderful!" said Lydie, and her brother, to Lisa's surprise, agreed with her.

"I thought the English were all cold and without passion, like the London fog," he said. "Giving up everything in chase of your heart is something which only we French would do. Are you sure that you are not French, Lisa?"

Grinning, Lisa shook her head.

"Then you must have French blood in you," he decided.

Lydie stood up. "And we are going to help you find your man!" she declared, and took the slip of paper on which was written Jean-Luc's address. "37 Rue de la Châtelaine," she read out.

"Do you know it," asked Lisa.

"Oui," she said. "It is only a few minutes' walk from here." She called the waitress over to pay the bill, and made for the door. "Come," she said to Lisa and Christophe.

"It's quarter-past seven in the morning!" Lisa protested. "We can't go yet!"

"Of course we can," said Lydie. "Don't be so English, my friend. When it is a matter of the heart then it is never too early!"

37 Rue de la Châtelaine was a seedy, run-down white stone building in a side street of Cannes, a stark contrast to the glamorous hotels and shops which Lisa, Lydie and Christophe passed on their way to Jean-Luc's flat. Many students lived here, Christophe explained to Lisa, taking advantage of the cheap rents and the friendly bohemian atmosphere.

They walked into the foyer of the block. Flat One was the first door on the left.

Lisa took a deep breath and looked at her two new friends. "How do I look?" she asked.

"You look beautiful, Lisa," Christophe assured her.

"Go on, Lisa, ring the bell," Lydie urged. "What are you waiting for?"

Because I'm nervous, Lisa thought. Because I don't know what reception I'm going to get. Will he be glad to see me? He still thinks that I two-timed him over James. Is he still hurt and angry?

And there was another nagging and even more worrying thought. What if he's not alone? It's been two months since I last saw him . . . What if he's forgotten about me? What if he's got a new girlfriend . . .?

"Ring the door bell, Lisa!"

Summoning up her courage Lisa pressed on the bell, and waited. There was no reply. She tried again. And again. Lisa looked hopelessly at Lydie and Christophe, as an old lady came out of the door of the opposite flat.

She said something to Lisa in a regional accent so strong and pronounced that Lisa had to look at Lydie for help.

"What did she say?" she asked.

"She says that Monsieur Roupie has left . . ." she said sadly. "That he arrived back from England two months ago, packed his things and left . . ."

Lisa felt the whole world spinning around. To have travelled hundreds of miles only to find that Jean-Luc had gone!

'Where's he gone to?' Lisa demanded urgently of Lydie. "Ask her where he's gone!"

"I'm sorry, Lisa," Lydie said sympathetically after she had posed the old woman the question. "Jean-Luc left no forwarding address . . ."

Lisa burst into tears and fell into Lydie's open arms.

22

Lisa sat on the balcony of Lydie and Christophe's holiday apartment, which overlooked the sparkling blue waves of the Mediterranean. She gazed morosely at the silver beaches crowded with bronzed and perfect bodies, at the water skiers and wind-surfers further out at sea. Down there people were enjoying themselves, probably having the time of their lives, she decided; it made a stark contrast to her own misery and anguish.

After Lisa had dried her tears, Lydie and Christophe had taken her to their apartment at the far end of the Croisette, the less trendy part where rents were cheaper. When Lisa told them that she had nowhere to stay that coming night they had offered to put her up on their floor. Lisa had responded with relief: when she had arrived in Cannes she had assumed that she would be staying with Jean-Luc; now with Jean-Luc gone a hotel room would eat quickly into the small amount of money she had saved from her summer job.

"What are you going to do, Lisa?" asked Lydie as she came out on to the balcony, carrying two glasses of freshly-squeezed orange juice.

"I have to find him, Lydie," she said as she stared at the palm-lined stretch of the Croisette, hoping against hope that she might suddenly see his distinctive green 2CV. "I love him. And he has to know the truth about me and James. If Alison hadn't lied to him we'd be together now."

"Do you have any clue as to where he might be?"

Lisa frowned and thought hard. Jean-Luc had told her a lot about his life in Cannes, but there was not one name she could recall. "I remember him telling me that his mother lived just outside Cannes. In a place called ... called ... Napou?"

"La Napoule," said Lydie. "I know it. It's about a twenty-minute bus ride from here ... Christophe, where are you going?"

Christophe returned to the balcony, with the Cannes telephone directory in his hand. "You may call me Sherlock Holmes, if you wish," he said and opened the book. With Lisa looking over his shoulder, he ran his finger quickly down the list of people with the surname Roupie.

"There's not one Madame Roupie who lives in La Napoule," Lisa said sadly. "What about looking up Jean-Luc Roupie?"

Lydie shook her head. "If he's just moved – and if he's still in the area – he wouldn't be in the telephone directory yet."

Lisa buried her face in her hands. "It's so hopeless," she wailed. "I'm never going to find him!"

Lydie pressed a soft and comforting hand on her new friend's. "Of course you will," she said. "You're more than just boyfriend and girlfriend, you're soulmates, so you told me, and soulmates belong together. They can never be apart for long."

"You really think so?"

"Of course we think so!" said Christophe. "And tonight you are going to get some rest. And the first thing tomorrow morning we are going to La Napoule!"

To the west of Cannes, La Napoule is a tiny town on the coast, which few tourists know about, preferring the more obvious attractions of the bigger city. Everyone seemed to know each other here and Lydie hoped that by asking around someone would be able to tell them where Jean-Luc's mother lived.

But as the day drew on it seemed that no one could help them. They asked in bars and cafés, they stopped pedestrians on the street, they even went down to the marina where the millionaires moored their yachts but no one had heard of a Madame Roupie whose only son Jean-Luc was a language student.

Lisa became more and more despondent. This is crazy she told herself. How can I possibly find him? I don't even know whether he's in Cannes or not. For all I know he could have gone and joined friends in Paris or somewhere else!

Even Christophe's regular words of encouragement didn't help to relieve her depression. As they sat together on the bus on the way back to Cannes Lisa began to seriously consider going back home.

"Don't give up hope," Christophe said. "You said he studied at Nice University."

"That's right."

"So we'll catch the train into Nice tomorrow. It's still the summer vacation but there will be students about. Perhaps some of them know where he is."

"You're both so kind," said Lisa. "Why are you doing all this for me?"

"Because we're French," smiled Lydie. "And there's nothing the French like better than a good love story."

She pointed out of the window of the bus, at a hang-glider in the air being pulled along by a speedboat.

Lisa watched the hang-glider swirl and soar in the darkening sky and marvelled at the man's courage: they'd certainly never get her up in one of those!

So intent was she on watching the hang-glider that Lisa completely missed the car which had just overtaken the bus travelling in the direction of Cannes.

It was a run-down and ramshackle green 2CV, driven by a certain dark-haired, brown-eyed Frenchman. And beside him in the passenger seat, her arm draped casually over his shoulder, was a stunningly beautiful and glamorous young woman.

23

Another wasted day followed in Nice, the big city about thirty minutes' train ride from Cannes. Lydie and Christophe knew some people at the university there and asked them about Jean-Luc. But as Lydie and Christophe, like Lisa, were science students, their friends also tended to be the same, and very rarely mingled with people like Jean-Luc who studied languages.

At noon they sat down at a small pavement café to have lunch. In front of them young people of both sexes in the latest fashions paraded, greeting friends, or just going to the large McDonalds in the city centre. (Whoever had decided that the French eat delicious haute cuisine all the time had never been to a French McDonalds at lunch-time, Lisa decided.) Everyone in the entire town seemed to know everyone else — every one, that was, except Jean-Luc Roupie!

As Lisa, Lydie and Christophe enjoyed their coffee, a girl of about Lisa's age came up to them.

"You are looking for Jean-Luc?" she asked in faltering English.

"Yes!" said Lisa, replying in French.

"I thought so. You were asking my friends about him earlier."

"Do you know where he is?" Lisa demanded, hope rising in her heart.

"No," the girl said, shaking her head, and Lisa's face fell.

"Have you any idea where he might be?" asked Lydie.

"All I know is that when he came back from England, he was very depressed and moody," the girl continued. "A girl, you understand, a thwarted affair of the heart . . ."

Lisa nodded sadly.

"He gave up his old flat, and no one has seen him for weeks," the girl concluded. "He could be anywhere now, anywhere at all . . ."

Lisa walked wearily along the Croisette as the sun set and the lights along the Croisette came on. Everywhere happy holiday-makers and locals, all dressed in the most chic clothes, cruised the famous boulevard with their friends – all intent on having a good time.

Christophe looked at Lisa and then at his own sister. Even Lydie was looking as despondent and maudlin as Lisa. In three days of searching for the elusive Frenchman all they had discovered was that his mother wasn't on the phone and that Jean-Luc had given up his flat. He was starting to think that it might be time for Lisa to admit defeat and go back to England and forget about Jean-Luc altogether.

"We need cheering up!" he announced grandly. "And I know just the thing! I'm buying us all a meal!"

"Christophe, that's sweet," Lisa said. "But you can't afford it . . ."

"And that is why I'm taking you to Vesuvio's!" he said.

"Vesuvio's?" asked Lisa. "What's that?"

"My favourite pizzeria on earth!" he explained. "The best pizzas in Cannes and at the lowest prices."

Vesuvio's was, in fact, one of the best-kept gastronomic secrets in the entire town. Located on the Croisette with a wonderful view of the beach and the Mediterranean, most tourists would pass by its unassuming façade and presume that it was just another pizzeria, one of thousands along the coast. But once they ventured inside they would find that the pizzas served there were huge and quite simply the most delicious this side of Italy. That was why at seven o'clock each evening there was always a long queue of locals waiting to be allowed in.

After a wait of about twenty-five minutes the three of them were let in and given a table in the corner of the restaurant. The pizzeria was packed with diners, and the waiters weaved their way in and out of the closely packed tables, holding the pizzas aloft on huge wooden platters.

Everywhere there was the delicious smell of freshly-baked dough mixed with the tangy aroma of cheeses and tomatoes, and home-grown basil. The air was a-buzz with the lively chatter of diners of all different nationalities, and the guttural accent of the waiters as they shouted their orders back to the busy kitchen. It was half-past seven, Vesuvio's had been open only half an hour and the place was already packed.

"See, I told you it was the best place in the whole of Cannes," said Christophe smugly. "Everyone who knows anything about the city comes here."

"There are just *so* many people," Lisa marvelled as she studied the comprehensive menu, wondering which one of Vesuvio's delicious pizzas to have. Christophe and Lydie had no need of menus: they were regulars here every summer and knew the menu off by heart.

When she had finally made her decision and Christophe had placed their order, Lisa looked around the restaurant. It seemed that the whole of Cannes from every social class and milieu had come to eat at the famous pizzeria.

To the table to the right of them was a group of four poor-looking students sharing two pizzas between them; behind the students there was a family table of two parents and their young children; over there was a beautiful sun-tanned couple, both of whom must surely be models, Lisa decided; and next to them an elderly man dining with his wife, whose ample bosom positively dripped with pearls, and whose long wrinkled fingers were covered with emeralds and rubies.

There was even a table of English tourists,

making a hopeless effort to place their order in French. Lisa smiled, as the waiter sighed theatrically, and replied to the tourists in faultless English.

And over in the far corner, through the hustle and bustle of the diners, and the waiters mincing their way through the crowds, was a young dark-haired man with his back to them. He was wearing a red Chevignon T-shirt which hung loosely from his smooth swimmer's shoulders; he was consulting the menu.

Lisa felt her breath cut short, and her whole body began to tremble with anticipation. She felt the blood rush to her head, and her heart began to pound.

She stood up suddenly, and Lydie and Christophe looked at her in concern.

"Lisa, what is it?" asked Lydie, but Lisa had already left their table and was fighting her way through the crowded tables of the pizzeria, ignoring the disgruntled complaints of the waiters or the curious stares of her fellow diners – to the table of the one man she'd thought she'd never see again. Lydie and Christophe followed her.

As she approached the table she felt her legs sinking beneath her. This was the moment she'd been living for – the moment she had been working for for two long and wretched months – the moment she had been looking forward to with all her heart.

It was also the moment she had most feared. The moment when he might turn around and laugh at her. The moment when she might discover that he'd found someone else. The moment when he wouldn't believe her, and when he would reject her, and walk out of her life for ever.

The moment when he wouldn't love her.

She took a deep breath.

"Hello, Jean-Luc. It's me – Lisa."

For a half-instant, unnoticed by everyone except Lisa, Jean-Luc paused. And then he turned around. The moment he saw Lisa his face broke into a wide smile, and he leapt out of his chair.

"Lisa!" he cried out, and reached out his arms to touch her, to see if she was real.

Lisa felt her entire heart go out to the only man she had loved, or would ever love. The joy on Jean-Luc's face was evident: even Lydie and Christophe, who had caught up with their friend, could see that now.

Jean-Luc was at a loss for words. "But what are you doing in Cannes?" he asked.

"I came looking for you," Lisa said brightly, scarcely able to contain her joy. "I tried to find you at your old flat but the lady there said that you'd moved . . ."

"Yes, I've moved in with—"

Suddenly Jean-Luc drew back suspiciously. Lisa's face darkened.

"You came looking for me?" he asked and there was a sneer on his face, as he tried unsuccessfully to forget the wrong he believed Lisa had done to him back in England. He glanced at the good-looking Christophe. "With your current boy-friend, I suppose?"

"Don't be stupid," said Lydie with uncharacteristic anger. "He's not Lisa's boyfriend! He's my brother!"

"You hurt me, Lisa, you don't know how much you hurt me," he said bitterly. "For the past two months I've been trying in vain to forget you; must you come back now and reopen all those old wounds? And now you are here, expecting me to forgive you?"

"I'm not asking you to forgive me, Jean-Luc," Lisa insisted.

"Oh no?"

"Because there isn't anything to forgive!" she declared.

For God's sake I know how you're hurting, she thought. How do you think I'm feeling? But put away your French masculine pride for a minute and listen to the truth!

"I was never two-timing you for James!"

Jean-Luc didn't say anything, just gave her a look of total disbelief. A look which said: And you expect me to believe that? After what Alison told me about the Christmas party? And after you stopped seeing me just as James came back from university?

"It was all a lie of Alison's so that she could get her claws into you!" she continued. "She fancied you something rotten, you know that! But I loved you! And I still do! And all I want in this world is for us to be happy. Together!"

Jean-Luc hesitated. What Lisa was telling him was something he fervently wanted to believe, but he had been made a fool of before and it had hurt his self-esteem very badly.

"Mon Dieu, monsieur!" said Christophe in exasperation. "Why would a girl come all the way from London to the South of France, if she wasn't in love with you?"

Now it was Jean-Luc's turn to look uncertain. And then, just as she thought her former boyfriend might believe her, Lisa's entire world fell apart.

There was a perceptible hush in the restaurant as the doors swung open and a tall and impossibly glamorous and sophisticated woman walked through the doors. She looked in her mid-twenties, with a mane of raven hair and dark-brown eyes. She was dressed in expensive designer clothes, and was as chic and as devastingly sexy as only Frenchwomen can be.

And every man in the restaurant couldn't take his eyes off her. Even Lisa realized that here was a woman so beautiful that she would make any supermodel look dowdy and plain.

The newcomer surveyed the restaurant, seemingly totally oblivious of the commotion and interest she had caused. Finally her eyes alighted on Jean-Luc and she strode over to him, the normally stroppy waiters making a path for her.

She planted a firm and loving kiss on Jean-Luc's lips. "Darling!" she said, in French, and placed her arm around his waist. "I'm sorry I'm late. But one of your friends called around at our flat, and — well, you know how it is, we started talking . . ."

Our flat?

Lisa felt herself trembling all over. Lydie and

Christophe looked at each other, acutely aware of what Lisa must be going through.

Our flat?

Jean-Luc coughed with embarrassment, and looked sheepishly at Lisa. "Er, Adrienne, can I introduce you to my friends . . ."

Adrienne smiled and held out her hand. "*Enchantée*," she said. "My name's Adrienne. And you are?"

"Lisa Tyler," Lisa said, choking back the tears which were already coming to her eyes.

Lisa Tyler, the girl who came all the way to the South of France to get back Jean-Luc. Not knowing that he's already living with his new girlfriend! And how could I – or anyone else, for that matter? – compete with someone as beautiful, as sophisticated, as glamorous and as self-assured as you?

What an idiot I've made of myself! she thought despairingly. To think that anyone like me could win the love of someone as gorgeous, as sexy and as wonderful as Jean-Luc. Why don't I just go back to England, back to James, and Applewood which is where I belong?

"Sorry, I didn't quite catch your name?" said Adrienne.

Lisa the Fool, Lisa the Hopeless, Lisa the Ridiculous, she thought as she ran out of the pizzeria, and out of Jean-Luc's life for ever.

24

The overnight train to Paris scrunched to a halt at the Gare de Lyon station at a quarter past six the following morning, and Lisa found herself once more stumbling across the station concourse, struggling with her heavy bag. She was bleary-eyed and though she was tired she hadn't slept a wink all night on the journey from Cannes to Paris. Outside the train station the rain was once more coming down in torrents.

After she had run out of the pizzeria Lydie had followed her and they had gone straight to Lydie's apartment, leaving a bemused Christophe to settle the bill. There Lisa had started furiously packing while Lydie looked on helplessly.

"I've made a total idiot of myself, Lydie," Lisa told her in French. "I travel all the way down to Cannes to look for him — and I find that he's already got himself a new girlfriend! And he says he was hurt when he thought I was two-timing him!"

"But, Lisa, perhaps she's only a friend," Lydie had suggested, although she didn't really believe it.

"Did you see the way she kissed him? The way she held him?" Lisa said scornfully. "I know we're in France but that's hardly the way that 'just good friends' behave, is it?

"No, Lydie, Jean-Luc was just a summer fling and I've got to learn to get over it . . ." she said, trying hard not to let her tears show.

Get over it? she thought despairingly. How can you get over the most wonderful, handsome, kind and charming man you have ever met in your whole life?

"What will you do?" asked Lydie. "You're welcome to stay here for the rest of the holidays."

"Thanks, Lydie, but no thanks," Lisa replied. "You and Christophe have been so kind to me, and I'll keep in touch. But the sooner I'm out of France, the better."

Because the sound of French being spoken, the people in the streets – even the smell of coffee and freshly-baked baguettes from the café – all remind me of the man I love.

Of the man I can never have.

"I'm getting the train back up to Paris and then to London," she revealed. "With any luck I'll be back home by tomorrow night."

"Won't your mother be suspicious?" asked Lydie. "You're supposed to be in Dorset for another week . . ."

Lisa shrugged. "I'll think of something," she said, and zipped up her bulging bag. She turned to Lydie and kissed her on the cheek. "Thanks for everything," she said.

"I hope you find happiness, Lisa," said Lydie as she dialled for a cab for which she insisted she would pay. "And I'm sure Christophe would too . . ."

"He's late . . ."

"Probably still arguing the bill at Vesuvio's," said Lydie. "But if I know my brother I wouldn't be at all surprised if he's telling Monsieur Roupie exactly what he thinks of him . . ."

Lisa looked around at the early-morning commuters arriving from the suburbs for work. They were all oblivious to her sadness, as they went about their individual lives, they were all so ignorant of the fact that her heart had been broken, and would never be whole again.

She sighed. No point in thinking about the past, she scolded herself. Must think about the future. A future at Applewood with 'A' levels next year. Who knows – James is a nice guy, after all. If Chrissie can fall for Simon maybe . . . She shook her head sadly, as a numbing realization fell on her: A future without Jean-Luc . . .

She bent down to pick up her bag. It was heavy and it was quite a struggle to lift it.

Suddenly, as though from out of nowhere, a hand appeared and grabbed hold of the strap.

"Allow me, mademoiselle," came a dark-brown voice, a voice Lisa thought she'd only ever hear again in her dreams.

She turned. "Jean-Luc?"

Jean-Luc was standing there, dressed in the clothes he had been wearing last night at the pizzeria. They were crumpled and creased and it looked as though he had slept in them all night; which, in fact, he had. He also hadn't shaved and the stubble on his chin made him look even sexier. He was looking at her with loving, hopeful eyes.

"I . . . I don't understand," Lisa babbled. What was Jean-Luc doing here in Paris when she'd just left him last night in the South of France?

"After you'd left, Christophe told me everything," Jean-Luc said. "All about Alison, and James, and how you came all the way down to Cannes to find me . . ."

"But how did you get here?" she asked.

"Last night I bought a ticket for the last flight from Nice to Paris," he explained. "I've been here all night just waiting for your train to come in . . ."

"How could you have afforded all that?" asked Lisa, her practical nature reasserting itself even now.

"Adrienne bought the ticket on her credit card," he said. "Otherwise I wouldn't have been able to afford it by myself."

Adrienne.

Lisa suddenly turned cold, anxious not to be made a fool of.

Adrienne.

"And who is Adrienne, then?" she demanded. "Your French girlfriend?"

Jean-Luc seemed surprised for an instant and then grinned.

And then smiled.

And then laughed fondly, adoringly, at Lisa.

"You thought Adrienne was my *girlfriend*?" he asked incredulously.

"Of course I did," said Lisa, suddenly feeling rather foolish.

"You crazy, crazy English girl," he said affectionately, and the love in his eyes for Lisa shone out. "Adrienne's not my girlfriend. Didn't I ever tell you that I have an older sister?"

"*Your sister?*"

Jean-Luc nodded and opened his arms wide. "That's right," he said. "Now come to me, Lisa. I don't ever want to let you out of my sight again."

Lisa fell into his embrace. She looked up into his eyes.

"I loved you, Jean-Luc," she said. "Even when I thought you had left me, even when I thought Adrienne was your girlfriend, I still loved you."

Jean-Luc looked down at her and stroked her hair. He kissed her on the forehead.

"And even when I thought you'd two-timed me, even when I told myself that I should never see you again, I knew that I loved you too. It hurt, but through all that hurt I knew that I still loved you, that you were the only one for me."

Lisa gazed dreamily into the deep brown eyes of the most gorgeous man in the world. "Soulmates?" she asked.

Jean-Luc nodded. "Soulmates," he confirmed. "And more than that. Lovers as well."

He held her tightly to him, so tightly that she hoped he would never let go. He kissed her, a long, passionate kiss which begged for forgiveness as much as expressing the love he felt for her.

Passers-by on their way to work stopped and stared at the young couple so obviously in love. Some tutted disapprovingly: others looked on admiringly. But Jean-Luc and Lisa didn't care; as far as they were concerned the rest of the world didn't exist.

Jean-Luc looked searchingly into her eyes, those baby-blue eyes that Lisa had once hidden behind her glasses.

He stroked her hair once more, that hair that she had once worn in a severe ponytail but now wore loose and free. He smiled.

"I'm not your teacher, Lisa," he whispered.

Lisa smiled too, and pressed herself even closer to her boyfriend's body. There were tears of delight in her eyes as she gazed up at his adorable face.

"And I'm not your student, Jean-Luc . . ."

Coming soon from Point Romance . . .

Two Weeks in paradise

by Denise Colby

Feeling light-headed, although she'd sipped only one glass of the champagne, Jackie clung tightly to Mason as they followed the crowd, shuffling heel to toe, along San Luis's main street towards La Plaza del Obispo. The old town square, with its decaying fountains pumping out light brown water, was dotted with palm-trees in which there perched dozens of brightly-coloured birds. On the far side of the square sat the only noteworthy building of the town – the Church of San Luis. Its walls had recently been cleaned and garlanded with exotic flowers: alamunda, anthuriums and wild orchids.

The noisy throng soon filled the square, all eyes on the church, children high up on their parents' shoulders, the smaller adults on tip-toe, peering across the taller heads which blocked their view.

At five o'clock precisely, the church bells began to sound out and this was immediately acknowledged by a throaty roar from the crowd. The roar subsided as the bells stopped ringing and an eerie silence fell on La Plaza del Obispo. The slow beat of a solitary drum resounded from the church and the crowd watched in awe as a bejewelled float, carried on the shoulders of the priests, made its way from the church portal and down the ramp towards them. Men, women and children, crossing themselves, parted as one, without taking their gaze from the float as they made an inroad, through which the priests could carry their burden.

On the float, hundreds of candles burned brightly around the seated diamond-studded figure of the Madonna, and as the priests marched slowly through the crowds in time to the beating drum, an infant, following on behind, his black face smiling through his white, priestly robes, proudly carried on a silver platter the reason for this fiesta – the gumbo.

The almost silent religious procession which had taken two hours to wind *its* way solemnly through the side streets of San Luis, finally returned to the church, the gumbo having been buried, laid to rest in El Jardin de Los Santos, the equivalent of a small, English park.

The carnival followed: steel bands beating out their hypnotic rhythms in the square, while rum-crazed adults and their excited offspring danced wildly with police and priests.

As it grew dark, everyone returned to El Jardin de Los Santos to watch los fuegos – a magnificent firework display, its loud bangs echoing through the narrow streets nearby and sounding like thunder. Mason pulled Jackie closer to him and held her tightly in his arms. And as the last rocket of the display shot high into the air, bursting and sprinkling the night sky with a thousand stars, he kissed her. And *that* was the kiss that she wished could go on and on for ever.